OUT WITH GUN AND CAMERA

or

The Boy Hunters in the Mountains

Captain Ralph Bonehill

1st WORLD
LIBRARY
Literary Society

Out with Gun and Camera

Captain Ralph Bonehill

© 1st World Library, 2006
PO Box 2211
Fairfield, IA 52556
www.1stworldlibrary.com
First Edition

LCCN: 2006936238

Softcover ISBN: 978-1-4218-3103-9
Hardcover ISBN: 978-1-4218-3003-2
eBook ISBN: 978-1-4218-3203-6

Purchase *"Out with Gun and Camera"*
as a traditional bound book at:
www.1stWorldLibrary.com/purchase.asp?ISBN=978-1-4218-3103-9

1st World Library is a literary, educational organization
dedicated to:

- Creating a free internet library of downloadable ebooks

- Hosting writing competitions and offering book
publishing scholarships.

Interested in more 1st World Library books?
contact: literacy@1stworldlibrary.com
Check us out at: www.1stworldlibrary.com

1st World Library Literary Society

Giving Back to the World

"If you want to work on the core problem, it's early school literacy."
- **James Barksdale, former CEO of Netscape**

"No skill is more crucial to the future of a child, or to a democratic and prosperous society, than literacy."

- **Los Angeles Times**

Literacy... means far more than learning how to read and write... The aim is to transmit... knowledge and promote social participation."

- **UNESCO**

"Literacy is not a luxury, it is a right and a responsibility. If our world is to meet the challenges of the twenty-first century we must harness the energy and creativity of all our citizens."

- **President Bill Clinton**

"Parents should be encouraged to read to their children, and teachers should be equipped with all available techniques for teaching literacy, so the varying needs and capacities of individual kids can be taken into account."

- **Hugh Mackay**

1st World Library Literary Society

Giving Back to the World

"If you want to work on the core problem, it's early school literacy."

- **James Barksdale, former CEO of Netscape**

"No skill is more crucial to the future of a child, or to a democratic and prosperous society, than literacy."

- **Los Angeles Times**

Literacy... means far more than learning how to read and write... The aim is to transmit... knowledge and promote social participation."

- **UNESCO**

"Literacy is not a luxury, it is a right and a responsibility. If our world is to meet the challenges of the twenty-first century we must harness the energy and creativity of all our citizens."

- **President Bill Clinton**

"Parents should be encouraged to read to their children, and teachers should be equipped with all available techniques for teaching literacy, so the varying needs and capacities of individual kids can be taken into account."

- **Hugh Mackay**

CONTENTS

PREFACE

My Dear Lads:

This story is complete in itself, but forms volume four in a line known by the general title of "Boy Hunters Series," taking in adventures with rod, rifle, shotgun and camera, in the field, the forest, and on river and lake, both in winter and summer.

My main object in writing this series of books is to acquaint lads with life in the open air, and cause them to become interested in nature. In the first volume, called "Four Boy Hunters," I told how the youths organized their little club and went forth for a summer vacation; in the second book, "Guns and Snowshoes," I gave the particulars of a midwinter outing, with its heavy falls of snow, its blizzard, and its most remarkable Christmas in the wilds.

With the coming of another summer the boys determined to go forth once more, and what they did then has been told in the third book, entitled "Young Hunters of the Lake." They had a glorious time, in spite of some enemies who tried to do them harm, and they settled the matter of certain "ghost" to their entire satisfaction.

The settling of the ghost question took them home before the summer vacation was half over, and then the boys began to wonder what they had best do next. But that question was soon answered by an announcement made by the father of one of the lads; and once again they went forth, this time, however, to the distant mountains. Here they hunted and fished to their hearts' content, and likewise took a large number of photographs, some of the pictures causing them a good deal of trouble and peril to obtain.

Trusting that all boys who love to hunt and to fish and to take pictures with a camera will find this volume to their liking, I remain, Your sincere friend, Captain Ralph Bonehill.

CHAPTER I

FRIENDS AND ENEMIES

"Come on, Shep."

"Where are you going, Whopper?"

"For a row on the river. I've been aching for a row for about a year."

"That suits me," answered Sheppard Reed, as he hopped down from the fence upon which he had been sitting. "What about the others?"

"Snap said he would meet me at the dock," continued Frank Dawson, otherwise known as Whopper. "I don't know where Giant is."

"I saw him about an hour ago. He was on an errand for his mother—said he was going to Perry's store."

"Then we can look in Perry's. If he isn't there I'll run over to his house for him. It's a grand day for a row."

"Yes, we must get him if we can," went on Sheppard Reed thoughtfully. "I've got something to tell the crowd."

"To tell the crowd?" repeated Frank Dawson curiously. "What?"

"I'll tell you when we are all together, Whopper."

"Something about Ham Spink? I met him last night and we almost had a fight. Oh, that dude makes me sick!"

"No, this isn't about Ham, or any of that crowd. It concerns— But I'll tell you later," and Sheppard Reed put on an air of great secrecy.

"All right. If you don't want to tell I suppose I'll have to wait," said Whopper disappointedly. "But you might tell me what's on your mind."

"I want to tell the whole crowd at once," answered his chum. "Then nobody can say somebody else was told first."

"I see. Well, you go down to the dock and meet Snap, and I'll hustle around and stir up Giant," went on Frank Dawson.

"I was going to have you all over to my house to-night, to tell you," explained Sheppard. "But I might as well speak of it when we are together on the river."

"Say, you must have something wonderful on your mind!" cried Whopper. "I'm dying by inches to know what it is. I'll find Giant somehow, and have him at the dock inside of a quarter of an hour sure." And away he ran on his errand, while the youth who had the important announcement to make turned in the direction of the water-front.

To those who have read the former volumes in this "*Boy Hunters Series*" the lads who have been speaking will need no further introduction. For the benefit of others let me state that Sheppard Reed was the son of a doctor who had a large practice in and around the town of Fairview. Shep, as he was usually called, was a bright and manly youth, and one who loved life out of doors.

Frank Dawson was a lad who had moved to the town some

years before, and by his winning manner had made himself many friends. The boy had a habit of exaggerating when telling anything, and this had earned for him the nickname of Whopper—even though Frank never told anything in the shape of a deliberate falsehood. As some of his friends said, "you could tell Frank's whoppers a mile off," which was a pretty stiff "whopper" in itself.

These two boys had two close chums, Charley Dodge, usually called Snap—why nobody could tell—and Will Caslette, known as Giant, because of his small stature. Charley, or Snap, as I shall call him, was the son of one of the richest men of the district, his father owning a part interest in a sawmill and a large summer hotel, besides many acres of valuable forest and farm lands. Giant was the son of a widow who had once been poor but was now in comfortable circumstances. Though small for his age, the lad was as manly as any of his chums, and they thought the world of the little fellow.

The town of Fairview was a small but prosperous community, located on the Rocky River, ten miles above a sheet of water known as Lake Cameron. The place boasted of a score of stores, several churches, a volunteer fire department, and a railroad station—the latter a spot of considerable activity during the summer months.

All of the boys loved to camp out, and about a year before this tale opens had organized an outing or gun club, as related in detail in the volume called *"Four Boy Hunters."* They journeyed to the shores of Lake Cameron and then to another body of water called Firefly Lake, and had plenty of fun and not a few adventures. During their outing they had considerable trouble with a dudish sport—from town named Hamilton Spink, and his cronies, and were in great peril from a disastrous forest fire.

When school opened the young hunters returned to their studies, but with the approach of the winter holidays their thoughts turned again to the woods and water, and once more they sallied forth, as related in full in "*Guns and Snowshoes.*" They found game in plenty, and also ran the perils of a great blizzard, and got lost in the snow.

"Shall we go out again?" was the question asked when the next summer vacation was at hand, and all answered in the affirmative. This time, as related in the volume called "*Young Hunters of the Lake,*" they ventured considerably farther from home—to the shore of a lake said to be visited by a much-dreaded ghost. There they again went hunting and fishing to their hearts' content, and once more had trouble with Ham Spink and his cronies. They saw the "ghost," and were at first badly scared, but in the end solved the awful mystery by proving that the "ghost" was nothing but a man—a relative of Giant, who had lost his mind and disappeared some time before. The man was restored to reason, and through his testimony Giant's mother obtained some money which had been tied up in the courts.

The finding of the man had brought the boy hunters back to Fairview before their summer vacation was half finished. What to do next was the question.

"We ought to go somewhere—staying at home is dead slow," was the way one of the lads expressed himself; but for a week or more nothing was done.

Whistling gaily to himself, Shep Reed hurried down to the lake front. As he came out on one of the docks he caught sight of Snap, surrounded by half a dozen other lads, all carrying various bundles, and all equipped with guns and fishing-rods.

"Ham Spink and his cronies," murmured the doctor's son to himself. "Wonder where they are bound?"

"Oh, we are going to have the outing of our lives this trip," Ham Spink was declaring in his usual lordly fashion. "It's going to be the finest outing ever started from this town."

"Where are you going?" asked Snap curiously.

"Do you suppose we are going to tell you?" demanded another boy, a lad named Carl Dudder. "Not much! We don't want you to come sneaking after us, to shoot the game that we stir up."

"We never sneaked after you," cried Snap rather indignantly. "And we have always been able to stir up our own game."

"Bah! I know better."

"Of course they have taken our game—more than once," came from Ham Spink. "And if they don't shoot our game they scare it off, so that we don't have a chance to bring it down."

"What you say, Ham Spink, is absolutely untrue, and you know it," put in Shep, brushing through the crowd. "We have never in our lives touched any game that was coming to you or your crowd. We—"

"Say, do you want to fight?" cried Ham Spink, working himself up into a quick passion; and he doubled up his fists as he spoke.

"No; but I can defend myself," answered the doctor's son just as quickly. "I am not afraid of you."

"And we are not afraid of ghosts, either," was Snap's sarcastic comment.

These last words made Ham Spink and one or two of his cronies furious. They had been up to the distant lake where the "ghost" had held forth, and had been so badly frightened that they had come home, "on the run," as Whopper expressed it now that the matter had been fully explained, Ham and his followers felt decidedly sheepish over it consequently, to mention the affair was as bad as to wave a red rag in front of a bull.

"You shut up about ghosts!" cried Ham, shaking his fist in Snap's face.

"Say, Ham, let us give 'em a dressing down before we leave," whispered Carl Dudder. He looked around the dock. "Nobody here but ourselves."

"That's the talk," put in another of the Spink crowd. "They deserve it for trying to crow over us."

Shep and Snap heard the talk and looked at each other. They endeavored to back away in the direction of the street, but before they could accomplish this the entire Spink crowd threw down their guns, rods and bundles and advanced upon them.

"Keep back!" cried the doctor's son.

"If you hit us you'll take the consequences!" added Snap.

An instant later Ham Spink and his cohorts closed in. Snap and Shep were caught, front and back, and several blows were quickly exchanged. It was an uneven contest, and the doctor's son and his chum might have fared badly had not a sudden cry rang out:

"Look at that, Giant! They are trying to maul Snap and Shep!" The cry came from Whopper.

"Let up there!" added Will Caslette. And then, as small as he was, he ran out on the dock and toward the center of the melee. Frank came with him, and each caught one of the Spink faction by the arm and swung him backward.

"Good! Here are the others!" panted Shep. "Give it to 'em, fellows; they started it!"

The arrival of the pair somewhat disconcerted the Spink crowd, and they stopped fighting. They were still six to four, but to handle four was only half as easy as to handle two. The others looked inquiringly at their leader.

"Give it to 'em!" muttered Ham; but even as he spoke he edged to the upper end of the dock, past Giant and Whopper.

"Give it to 'em yourself," murmured a follower who had received a blow in the eye. "I guess I won't fight any more to-day."

As quickly as it could be done, Whopper and Giant ranged alongside of Snap and the doctor's son. They gazed defiantly at the crowd that confronted them. For a brief spell there was an ominous silence.

"Say, did we come here to fight or to start on our outing?" asked a lad of the Spink crowd. He was tall and thin, and evidently very nervous. He was a newcomer in the town and knew but little about the quarrels of bygone days.

"Don't waste time here," added another youth. "We can finish with them when we come back."

"You are afraid, now that we are four to six," said Snap. "You were willing enough to pitch into Shep and me when we were alone."

"Oh, give us a rest!" growled Ham Spink, not knowing what else to say. He caught up the things he had been carrying. "Come on, fellows," he added, and almost ran from the dock.

With great rapidity, for they were afraid Snap and his chums would charge upon them, the others of the Spink coterie took up their guns, rods and bundles and followed their leader.

"Let us go after 'em!" cried Whopper. "We can knock them into the middle of next Christmas, and I know it!"

"That's the talk!" cried the plucky Giant. "Let's go and make mincemeat of 'em!" And he started to follow those who had retreated.

"No use, boys!" called out Snap. "Come back."

"Why not?" demanded Whopper.

"They are going aboard the *Mary Raymond*. Ham said so. There she is now, with a lot of other passengers. See, they are heading for that dock already."

"Where are they going, anyway?" asked Giant as he halted.

"I know," whispered Whopper. "Just heard about it. They are going to camp out behind Lake Narsac, in the Windy Mountains."

"The Windy Mountains?" ejaculated the doctor's son in evident astonishment. "Did you say the Windy Mountains, Whopper?"

"I did. Why, what's the matter, Shep?"

"Well, if that don't beat the Dutch!" And then Shep shook his head in a manner that indicated something did not suit him at all.

CHAPTER II

ANOTHER OUTING PROPOSED

"Will you be so highly condescending and much obliging as to open the trapdoor of your mind and let us know what it is that beats the Dutch?" demanded Giant, after he and his chums had looked at the doctor's son for several seconds in silence.

"Why, yes, of course," answered Shep. "But er—it all fits in with what I was going to tell you about in the first place."

"And that was—" burst out Whopper eagerly.

"Wait till we are out on the river, away from the town folks. I don't want everybody to know our business."

"Great Scott! but Shep's got a secret!" burst out Snap. "What is it—a treasure hunt, or a new way to make diamonds?"

"Now quit fooling, and come on out in the boat, and you'll soon know all about it," replied the doctor's son.

"Then we have got to wait?" asked Giant reproachfully.

"And when we are dying by inches to know," added Whopper.

"Yes, you've got to wait. So the sooner we get out on the river the better—if you are dying, as you say," responded the doctor's son.

While talking the four chums had been watching the departure of the Ham Spink crowd from another dock. Soon the boat that carried the dudish bully and his cronies disappeared around a bend of the river.

In a very few minutes Shep and his chums had their rowboat out. They were used to rowing together, and each took his accustomed place at the oars. Shep gave the word, and like clockwork four blades dropped into the water and the rowboat shot away from the dock.

"Where shall we go?" asked Giant.

"Let us row over to Lackney's orchard," answered Snap. "Dandy apples there—and Mr. Lackney told me we could help ourselves."

"Suits me!" cried Whopper. "I'd rather eat apples than go to a fire. Us three can eat while Shep does the spouting."

"Humph! perhaps I'd do a little eating myself," came from the doctor's son.

It was an ideal day in midsummer, and all of the lads were in the best of spirits. As they rowed along they discussed the encounter with the Spink faction.

"I wish they'd leave us alone," was Shep's comment. "I am getting so I fairly hate the sight of Ham and Carl Dudder."

"So do I," added Whopper. "But they don't intend to leave us alone, and that is all there is to it."

"I am sorry they are going up into the Windy Mountains," said Shep. "It will—" And then he stopped short.

"Say, Shep, if you keep on like that we'll pitch you overboard," cried Whopper. "If you've got anything to tell, tell it, or else keep still."

"Wait till we get to Lackney's orchard," was all the doctor's son would reply.

They soon came to a bend in the river and, crossing here, drew up to a spot where some trees and bushes overhung the water. All leaped ashore and Snap tied the craft fast to a stake. Then the chums strolled up to some near-by apple trees, selected some fruit that suited them, and threw themselves on the ground to enjoy their feast.

"Now we are ready to listen to your imperial majesty's secret," observed Giant as he munched a juicy apple.

"Yes, let us in on it, by all means," added Snap.

"And don't say it's about lessons for the coming fall," put in Whopper with a mock-serious look.

"Lessons!" burst out Giant. "Perish the thought!"

"Well, to start with," began the doctor's son. "How would you like to go camping again?"

"Fine!"

"Great!"

"Couldn't be better!"

"Just as I thought," continued Shep. "And just what I told my father. He wants us to go out, you know," and Shep's eyes began to twinkle.

"He wants us to go out?" asked Whopper. "You mean he is willing for you to go?"

"No, he told me to ask you if you wanted to go out—for him."

"Mystery on mystery," came from Giant. "For him? I don't understand."

"Neither do I," came simultaneously from Snap and Whopper.

"Will, it's this way, to tell you the whole story. Can you keep a secret?"

"Of course!"

"Well, then, my father has become interested in a big land company that has procured a large reservation of land in and along the Windy Mountains. The company isn't going to do much with the reservation this year, but next year it is going to build camps up by the lake, and advertise it as a sort of private hunting and fishing resort. They hope to get the better class of sportsmen up here from the cities and make considerable money."

"Yes; but how does that affect us?" asked Giant impatiently.

"Wait and you'll see. My father says the success of the scheme will depend very largely on how it is presented to the public, and he and two of the other men have decided to do some high-class advertising of the project—little booklets and folders, and all that. These booklets and folders are to be filled with photo-engravings, showing the pretty spots in the mountains, and also pictures of the animals and fish a sportsman can get."

"And does your father want us to get the photographs?" asked Snap.

"That's it—if we care to do it. He can't go out, and neither can those other men, and they don't know who to get. Of course, they could hire a professional photographer, but he would only take scenery, most likely, while what my father wants particularly is pictures of good hunting and fishing, and pictures of real camp life. He thinks we are just the boys to get the right kind of pictures—"

"So we are, if we had the right kind of cameras," broke in Whopper.

"Yes; give me a high-class camera and plenty of films or plates, and I'll take all the photos he wants," added Snap.

"I haven't got to the end of my story yet," resumed the doctor's son. "Father knows that the pictures—I mean the right kind—will be worth money, and so he said, if we'd go out, and do the very best we could about getting the photos, he would furnish the cameras and plates, and would pay all the expenses of the trip."

"Whoop! hurrah! that suits me down to the ground!" cried Whopper. "Let's start to-morrow—no, this afternoon!"

"Offer accepted with pleasure," came from Giant.

"Do you really think we can get the photographs your father wants, Shep?" asked Snap. "It wouldn't be fair to take the offer up and then disappoint him."

"He thinks we can do it. He says he will get us the proper outfit, and before we start he'll have a professional photographer, who has made a study of landscapes, give us pointers on how to get the best results. He knows we can take pretty good pictures already."

"In that case, I say, let us accept the offer, by all means," answered Snap.

"How soon can we start?" demanded Whopper.

"I asked my father that, and he said most likely by next Monday. He will want to give us all some instructions before we leave. And he wants us to read this book," and Shep drew a small volume from his pocket.

"What is it?"

"A book on how to take the best photographs of wild animals."

"Humph! It's easy to get a picture—if you can find the animal," was Whopper's comment.

"This tells how to get a picture if you can't find the animal."

"What!"

"Exactly. Here are diagrams showing how to rig up a camera and a flashlight, so that if the animal comes along in the dark and shoves a certain string the light goes off and so does the camera, and the picture is taken. If you want to, you can bait the string."

"Say, that's great!" cried Giant.

"I'd like to lay the game low—after I had the picture," was Snap's comment.

"We can do that, too—sometimes."

After that the doctor's son gave his chums more details of what his parent had said. All the boys were sure they could go out again, for their return home from their previous trip had not been expected by their parents.

"Were you thinking we might meet Ham Spink and his crowd?" asked Giant during a short lull in the talk.

"Yes," answered Shep. "And if we do, they'll sure try to make trouble for us."

"I am not afraid of them," said Snap. "If they don't keep their distance we'll—"

"Give 'em as good as they send," finished Whopper. "But great

Caesar's tombstone! just think of going camping again!" And in his joy the youth turned a handspring on the grass. As he arose Giant threw an apple core that took him in the ear. Then Whopper threw a core in return, hitting Shep. A general fusillade of cores followed, and the lads ended by chasing each other around the orchard. Then they trooped back to the rowboat.

"Shall we go and talk to your father?" asked Snap on the way back.

"I think he'd like it if you would," answered the doctor's son. "I'll see if he is disengaged."

Dr. Reed was busy with a lady caller and the boys had to wait a quarter of an hour. Then he came into the sitting-room and shook hands warmly.

"So you are willing to undertake the commission to get pictures, eh?" he said after a few words. "Well, I am glad of it, for I know you can do it if you'll try. The outing ought to just suit you."

"It certainly will," answered Snap.

"I'll get the cameras at once and likewise the other things. Let me see, what cameras have you now?"

The boys told him, and he made some notes in a book. A general talk followed, and the physician told the lads just what he would like best to have. He cautioned them to keep quiet concerning the land company's projects.

"We want to spring this on the general public as a surprise," he explained. "If we don't keep it quiet some other folks may try to get ahead of us. To my mind our section of the Windy Mountains is an ideal one for city sportsmen, being wild and yet not too wild, and having some charming spots for camping."

"And hunting and fishing ought to be good," added Whopper. "I've heard Jed Sanborn say so." Jed Sanborn was an old hunter who knew every foot of territory for miles around the river and its lakes.

"I suppose we can take along the same general outfit we had before," remarked Whopper.

"I will get you a new and larger tent," answered the doctor, "and a few other things I think you ought to have." Can you go to Rallings to-morrow?"

"Rallings?" asked several.

"Yes. I will pay your way. I want you to go to visit Mr. Jally, the photographer. He is the one to give you a few lessons in photography."

The boys could all go, and it was decided to visit Railings early in the morning. The physician said he would give his son a letter of instructions for the photographer.

"It would be a good thing if you could stay overnight," said Dr. Reed. "Then you could have two days instructions instead of one. You could stay at my sister's house."

"That would be jolly!" cried Shep. He loved his aunt and knew she would make him and his chums welcome.

"I guess I can stay—anyway, I'll find out," answered Snap; and Giant and Whopper said the same.

Little did any of the boys dream of what strange happenings that visit to Railings was to bring forth.

CHAPTER III

A LESSON IN PHOTOGRAPHY

By consulting a time-table the boys found that a train for Railings left at ten minutes after eight in the morning. The distance to the city was thirty-three miles and the run on the country railroad took the best part of an hour and a quarter.

Snap, Whopper and Giant were on hand ten minutes before train time. They found the doctor's son ahead of them, and he had tickets for all.

"Well, how did you make out at home?" was the question asked by several, and then it was learned that all had had an easy time of it persuading their parents to let them go on the proposed outing to the Windy Mountains.

"My folks told me to beware of ghosts," said Snap with a grin.

"We needn't beware if the ghost turns out to be like that other," answered Giant.

"My folks told me to keep out of trouble especially with Ham Spink's crowd," said Whopper.

"Say, fellows, I reckon you have forgotten something," said Shep.

"Forgotten something?" queried Whopper.

"Exactly."

"What?"

"There's a circus at Rallings—to-day and tomorrow."

"Why, so there is!" exclaimed Giant. "How queer we didn't remember it before! Casso's United Railroad Shows. Do you suppose it is worth going to see?"

"I don't know. But as the admission is only twenty-five cents we might take it in—if we get the chance."

"Oh, let us take it in, by all means," pleaded Whopper. "Why, I'm dying to see the elephants and acrobats and all that!"

"Seems to me you're dying pretty often lately," answered Snap with a smile. "You ought to become a dyer by trade!" And then he ducked as Whopper made a playful pass at his head.

When the train came along the lads found it well filled, mostly with country folks going to Rallings to see the circus. They had to stand up part of the distance to the city.

"Maybe the photographer will be so busy he won't want to bother giving us lessons," said Snap.

"Maybe," answered the doctor's son. "We'll have to take our chances."

Reaching Rallings, the boys hurried at once to the studio of the photographer. They found Mr. Jally taking a family group of father, mother and three sons, and had to wait until the sitting was over. While they waited they watched the crowds on the street.

"Going to be plenty of folks here to see the circus," was Snap's comment, and his words proved true, folks flocking in from every quarter of the surrounding districts.

When Mr. Jally was at liberty he read Dr. Reed's letter with interest.

"The doctor mentioned this to me when he was in Rallings last Saturday," said the photographer. "I said I'd do what I could for you lads. I am sorry it is circus day, as I am likely to be busy. But I'll give you all the time I can spare."

"We can come to-morrow, too," said Shep. "We are going to stay in Rallings over night."

"Good! I think I can give you quite a few pointers in that time. I believe you all know something about photographs already."

"Yes; here are some of our snapshots," said the doctor's son, and he brought forth the pictures the boys had taken on their various outings.

"These are not bad," pronounced the photographer after an examination. "Some of them are very good. They indicate that you have it in you to take some good pictures." And then he went over the prints carefully one by one, telling them which seemed to be under exposed and which over, and which had not been properly developed and printed. Then he went into the question of grouping and centering and focusing, and told them how best to time their exposures. He was interrupted twice by girls who wanted their pictures taken, and then he told them a great deal about the values of lights and shades, and about suitable backgrounds. Then he brought forth an album of outdoor views and told them to study what was written under each picture.

"There is the time of day and the day of the month," he said, "and also the condition of the weather. These figures show the 'stop' of the shutter, and these the length of the exposure. Have you a timecard for exposures?"

"No; but we are going to get one," answered Shep.

"They are quite valuable; but even with a card one must often use his own judgment as to just what stop to use and how much time. If you are particularly anxious about a picture you had better take two or three exposures of it, instead of only one. Even the best of photographers occasionally fail to get good results on a first trial."

After that Mr. Jally brought forth several cameras he had used in outdoor work and explained how they might be used to the best advantage in taking different kinds of pictures and under various conditions.

"Strange as it may seem," he said, "no two scenes can be handled alike. In one the background may be very light and in the other very dark. One day the atmosphere may be very clear, the next it may be very dense."

"Yes, we know that, and we have found out that clouds over the sun make a big difference," said Snap.

The boys spent the balance of the morning and nearly all of the afternoon with the photographer, and learned many things of which they had been formerly ignorant. He recommended that they purchase and study several books on photography, and this they agreed to do.

"I see by the letter that Dr. Reed wishes me to pick out your cameras," said Mr. Jally. "I am going to the city Saturday and will get them and leave them at the doctor's house Saturday evening."

"And will you get the films and plates and other things, too?" questioned Whopper.

"Yes. The doctor wants a complete outfit, including a daylight developing tank, and all the chemicals for developing and printing. Then you can see what your pictures look like before you leave camp, and if a picture doesn't suit you can take it over again."

"Not if it's a wild beast," answered Giant with a grin.

"In the case of wild animals you had better save your films or plates until you get home. Developing in camp is not conducive to the best work, and you might lose the very film or plate you wanted the most."

"Yes, I know something about that," said Whopper. "I once took a beautiful picture—at least, I thought it was beautiful— of a flock of sheep, and when I tried to develop the plate in a hurry I got one end light-struck, so it was no good."

"Yes, and once, when I was in a hurry to develop a roll of films I had of a military parade," said Snap, "I got the hypo in the tank instead of the developing solution, and that was the end of that roll."

"This is a good rule to remember," said the photographer. "Never open the shutter of your camera until you are certain you are ready to take the picture, and never attempt to develop a plate or a film until you are sure your chemicals are properly mixed, and until you are sure you have everything at hand with which to work, and until you are sure the plate or film is properly protected from the light."

The boys were surprised when Mr. Jally announced that it was supper time and that he must go home.

"Gracious! And I told my aunt we'd be to supper by six o'clock!" exclaimed Shep. "We'll have to leg it to her house."

"Come again to-morrow at nine o'clock," said the photographer, and this the chums promised to do.

"Well, I've learned a whole lot to-day," said Snap as they walked along. "I am sure I can take a much better picture than formerly."

"And I've learned one little lesson," came from Whopper.

"After this I am not going to take so many snapshots of landscapes. I am going to take time exposures, and put my camera on a tripod, and study the scene through the ground glass, to get the best view possible."

Mrs. Carson, the doctor's sister, had given the boys their dinner, and now she had supper on the table waiting for them. Their experiments of the afternoon had made them hungry, and all "pitched in" with a vigor that made the good woman smile.

"What do you intend to do this evening?" she asked.

"We are going to the circus, Aunt Jennie," answered Shep. "Father said we might go."

"I thought as much. Don't stay out too late."

"We'll come home as soon as the show is over."

"Well, if it gets too late I'll put the key out for you—under the front-door mat," said Mrs. Carson. "I fancy you can find your way to your rooms."

"Certainly," answered Snap.

"You needn't stay up for us, Aunt Jennie," said Shep, who knew his relative was in the habit of retiring early.

"I am not going to bed so very early, Shep. I am afraid some of those tramps who follow the circus will come and rob me. I heard the town was full of the good-for-nothings."

"You had better lock up good after we are gone," said Giant.

"No fear but what I'll do that," answered Mrs. Carson.

"We'll try not to wake you up when we come in, aunty."

"I'll hear you, never fear. And, Shep, if you are hungry when you get back, you'll find a jar of cookies in the pantry, and a pitcher of milk in the icebox."

"Good for you!" cried the doctor's son, and he ran around the table and gave his aunt a hug and a kiss. "You know what boys like, don't you?"

The four chums were soon on their way to the circus grounds, located on the outskirts of Railings. Here they found erected a large main tent and several smaller ones, all lit up by numerous gasolene torches. At one side of the main tent was a side show, with numerous pictures hung between high poles. Near the entrance to the big show was a ticket wagon, and here a long line of people were awaiting their turns to get the bits of pasteboard which would admit them to the wonders under the canvases.

"Going to have a big crowd and no mistake," observed Snap as he looked at the folks flocking to the circus grounds.

"I heard they had a big crowd this afternoon, too," said Giant.

"They had a big crowd and a big fight," said a man standing near.

"A fight?" queried Whopper.

"Yes. It's a wonder somebody wasn't killed."

"What was the fight about?" questioned the doctor's son.

"Why, it seems the head boss of the show discharged four of the wagon drivers for drunkenness. The fellows wanted their full month's wages and the boss wouldn't give it to them. Then they got ugly and commenced to tamper with some of the animals. The boss called some of his other men, and all hands had a big fight right in the menagerie tent. One boy who was looking on got hit with a club, and a lady fainted, and they almost had a panic. Then the police took a hand, and one of the fellows who was discharged was arrested. The other three got away."

"Yes, and those other three men say they are coming back," said a farmer who stood near and who had overheard the conversation. "I saw them at supper time, back of Lum's hotel. They say they are going to get square on the circus boss, even if they have to break up the whole show to do it."

"I hope they don't come back to-night," said Snap. "I don't want to get mixed up in any quarrel."

"Me either," answered the farmer. "I want to see the show, and that's all."

"I don't think they'll come back," said the first man who had spoken. "If they did the police would arrest them on sight. They'll go to the next town and lay for the circus there."

By this time the boys had worked their way up to the ticket wagon. Each purchased a ticket of admission, and a moment later all passed on to the inside of the main tent.

CHAPTER IV

WHAT HAPPENED AT THE CIRCUS

The lads had not seen a circus for two years, consequently the show had much of the air of novelty about it for them. They spent half an hour in the menagerie tent, inspecting the wild animals, and then took seats in the main tent, as close to the rings as they could get. Casso's United Railroad Shows was quite an affair, and the performance was given in two rings at a time, as well as upon a trapeze in the air between the tent poles.

First there was the usual procession of horses and riders, elephants and camels, ponies and carts and racing chariots, and then came the acts, all of more or less thrilling interest. There were six clowns, and they kept the audience in a roar of laughter.

"Say, this is an all-right show," remarked Giant, after witnessing some particularly thrilling bareback riding. "I wouldn't try to do that trick on horseback for a thousand dollars."

"Here come the acrobats," said Snap as four bespangled performers ran into the rings and bowed and kissed their hands. Then the acrobats climbed up to two bars and did various "turns," all more or less hazardous.

"Here comes a boy!" cried Shep, as another performer stepped into one of the rings and bowed.

"Just look how thin and pale he is," whispered the doctor's son, who sat not far away from the youthful acrobat.

"Looks as if he had had a spell of sickness," added Giant.

The youthful acrobat did look as if he had been sick and was not yet entirely over it. He walked slowly over to one of the ropes and grasped it in his thin, white hands.

"I—I can't go up, Mr. Jones," the chums heard him whisper to the ringmaster.

"Yes, you can—and will, or I'll cut you with the whip!" was the ringmaster's harsh answer, and he cracked his lash loudly.

"I—I'm not well enough yet—my head is dizzy," pleaded the young acrobat.

"Up you go!" snarled the ringmaster, and cracked his whip in such a fashion that the end of the lash took the young acrobat in the calf of the leg, causing him to cry with pain.

"What an outrage!" whispered Snap, clenching his fists. "That ringmaster ought to be cowhided."

Painfully the young acrobat started to pull himself up on the rope. The ringmaster glared at him and then cracked his whip once more, taking the young performer in the arm.

"Shame! shame!" cried Snap; and "Shame!" added the other boys quickly.

"Shut up, you boys!" growled the ringmaster, turning quickly.

"Then let that boy alone," answered Snap loudly.

"If you don't shut up I'll have you put out!" roared

the ringmaster.

The young acrobat had climbed the rope a distance of ten feet. Now he appeared to grow dizzy, and of a sudden he lost his grip and fell in a heap in the sawdust ring.

"You rat, you, I'll fix you!" hissed the ringmaster. "What do we pay you for, anyway?"

He raised his long lash again, but before he could bring it down Snap and Shep leaped from their seats, quickly followed by Giant and Whopper and two well-dressed men.

"Don't you hit that boy," cried Snap loudly. "Don't you do it!"

"That's right—let the kid alone," added one of the well-dressed men.

"Go back to your seats—this is none of your affair," growled the ringmaster.

"It is our affair," put in the doctor's son. "That boy is sick—everybody can see it. He can't perform."

He purposely spoke in a loud voice, so that many heard him. At once a murmur arose on all sides.

"That's right—the kid is sick—take him out of the ring."

"It's an outrage to try to make him perform."

"The Society for the Prevention of Cruelty to Children ought to look into this."

Half a hundred men and boys stepped up to the ring, and for a few minutes the discussion waxed warm. In the meantime the young acrobat arose unsteadily to his feet. He was so weak he could hardly stand.

"Get back to the dressing-room, and be quick about it," growled the ringmaster to him. "I'll settle with you for this later."

"Down that ringmaster! Give him his own lash!" came from a burly farmer. "We'll teach him to abuse a boy as is sick!"

This cry was taken up by several. Growing alarmed, the ringmaster took to his heals and disappeared in the direction of the dressing-tent, whence his young victim had already gone. Then the band struck up, and the manager of the show sent out the clowns to do an extra stunt to quiet the audience.

"I'm afraid that ringmaster will have it in for that boy," said Snap to his chums.

"Poor boy!" murmured the doctor's son. "He didn't look as if he was used to this hard life. I wish we could do something for him."

"Let us try to look into the dressing-room and see what is going on," suggested Snap.

The four boys watched their chance, and walking around the main tent, crawled under some slanting seats and then got close to the canvas that divided the main tent from that used by the performers in "making up."

"Grandy, you must know what became of the little rascal," they heard the ringmaster say. "He came in here."

"So he did, sir," was the answer of a canvasman. "But he didn't stay. He just caught up some clothing and dusted."

"What! Ran away?"

"He dusted. I don't know where he went."

"Humph! He wouldn't dare to run away. If he tries that game

I'll take his hide off when. I catch him."

"He couldn't run very far, Mr. Jones—he was too weak."

"Bah! He isn't sick. He wants to shirk his act, that's all. Just wait till I get hold of him—I'll teach him to get me into hot water with the audience!" fumed the ringmaster.

"Well; I don't know where he went," answered the canvasman, and resumed his work on the wall of the menagerie tent. Then the ringmaster walked to another part of the dressing-tent to put on his street clothing, for he did not dare appear in the ring again at that performance.

"I hope that boy did run away," said Snap as he and his friends turned back to look at the rest of the performance. "I don't see why such a nice looking lad should travel with such a crowd as this."

"Oh, I suppose some of the circus folks are good people," answered Whopper. "But not that ringmaster."

"He ought to be tarred and feathered, and I'd like to help do it," came from Giant.

"Wonder who the boy is?" asked Shep.

"He is down on the bills as Master Buzz, the Human Fly. Of course, Buzz isn't his real name."

"No. It is more likely to be Smith or Jones," answered Whopper. "I'd like to see him and have a talk with him."

"Perhaps we'll get a chance to-morrow. The circus is to stay two days, you know," said Snap.

"Maybe the boy is all alone," said Shep. "If he is it might be that he would like it first rate if we would help him."

The boys had lost interest in the show, and were not sorry when it came to an end. They were among the first out, and hurried directly toward Mrs. Carson's house. In doing this they had to cross the railroad track, and here a passing freight train held them up. The freight came to a halt, and backed to take on some empties. Then it proceeded slowly on its way.

"Well, I never!" cried Snap suddenly as one of the empty cars came into view, under the rays of an electric light. "Look there!"

He pointed to the open doorway of a car. A figure stood there, wrapped in a coat several sizes too large for it—the figure of a slender boy with a whitish face,

"Was that that boy acrobat?" gasped Whopper as the freight train gathered headway and cleared the crossing.

"I think it was," answered Snap.

"So do I," put in the doctor's son.

"If it was, he is losing no time in getting out of town," was Giant's comment. "And I don't blame him."

"He had on a coat big enough for a man, and his trousers were rolled up around his feet," observed Snap. "Most likely he grabbed up the first suit he could find when he left the dressing-tent."

"If it really was the boy," said Whopper. "It looked like him, but we may be mistaken."

It did not take the four youths long to reach Mrs. Carson's home. They went in softly, and each got a cookie and a drink of milk. Then they went to bed and slept soundly until morning.

Promptly on time they presented themselves at Mr. Jally's

studio, and found not only the photographer but also an assistant present.

"I am going to leave my assistant in charge," said Mr. Jally. "I'll go out with you, and we'll have a practical lesson in getting outdoor views."

Taking two cameras with them, the photographer and the boys started off, to be gone until noon. They walked across the city and along the river, and at the latter locality took half a dozen pictures, Mr. Jally instructing them all the while.

"Now I'll show you how a commonplace bit of scenery can be made to look quite romantic," said Mr. Jally presently. "Let us walk over to the railroad embankment. Such an embankment is not pretty in itself, but I think we can get quite a pretty view of it."

After many instructions they took a view of the embankment. Their walk had tired the photographer, who was rather stout, and he proposed that they rest. Near at hand was a section shed with some lumber piles, and there they took it easy.

During a lull in the conversation the boys noticed three men approaching. They were rather tough-looking characters, and at first the lads took them to be tramps. The men walked behind the lumber piles without noticing our friends.

"Some fellows that followed up the circus, I suppose," said Snap.

"Yes; the kind my aunt was afraid of," added the doctor's son.

"We can do it jest as well as not," they heard one of the men say. "An' we got a right, too."

"Sure we got a right," said another of the trio in a heavy, rasp-like voice. "We'll show Casso what it means to do a feller out o' his lawful wages."

"Yes; but you look out you ain't caught," added the third man. "He's got all hands watching to spot us."

"We'll bust up his show, see if we don't," growled the first speaker.

"They must be the fellows who were discharged for drunkenness," whispered Snap.

"Yes; and they are laying plans to square up with the proprietor," added Whopper. "Wonder what they will do?"

"If they are up to anything unlawful, they ought to be exposed," was Mr. Jally's comment. He, too, had heard of the quarrel of the afternoon before.

"I don't care to put myself out to help that circus man," said Snap. "He is responsible for what happened to that sick boy. At the same time, I know 'two wrongs don't make a right.'"

The men continued to talk, but in such low tones that the others could only catch a word or two. Something was said about a lion and a chimpanzee and a toolhouse, but the boys could not imagine what the circus men had in mind to do.

Presently one of the circus men got up from his seat and walked around the lumber piles. When he saw the boys and Mr. Jally he uttered a whistle of surprise. Then he turned back to his companions, and all three of the men hurried away into the woods skirting the railroad tracks.

CHAPTER V

SOMETHING ABOUT A LION

"They are certainly up to something," was Snap's comment.

"Yes; and I'd give something to know just what it is," added the doctor's son.

Having rested, Mr. Jally took the boys to the bank of the river and there showed them how to make a good picture with a strong reflection in the water. This was rather difficult because of the distribution of light over the plate.

"Be careful when you point your camera toward the sun," said the photographer. "Otherwise you may get a sun-spot, or 'ghost,' right in the center of your picture."

"I know about that," said Whopper. "Once I tried to take a picture of my cousin standing by a well. The glare of the sun got on the plate just where her head ought to have been, so she was headless."

"That sure was a ghost!" cried Shep; and then all laughed.

The boys were to take the seven o'clock train back to Fairview, so at five o'clock they bid farewell to Mr. Jally and walked toward Mrs. Carson's house to get supper. Just as they turned the corner of a street close to the house they heard a man yelling wildly. He was running rapidly at the same time.

"What's that fellow saying?" asked Whopper. "Maybe it's a fire."

"No, he didn't say fire," returned Snap. "It sounded to me like lion."

"Lion?" questioned Whopper.

"Look out for the lion!" bawled the man. "Look out for the lion!" And down the street he went on the double-quick.

"He did say lion!" exclaimed Giant.

"One of the circus lions must have gotten free!" burst out the doctor's son.

"Or else those circus men let him loose!" returned Snap. "Don't you remember they said something about a lion?"

"So they did."

Others were now taking up the cry, and in a very few minutes men, women and children were hurrying in all directions to get out of the way of the beast. Some said it was one lion, and some said five or six, and everybody was thoroughly scared.

"We'll be eat up alive!" shrieked one lady. "Come, Bess!" And she took her little girl by the hand and ran for home, slamming and locking the door after her.

Soon everybody was running for shelter, and in a twinkling the doors of stores and houses were tightly closed, and windows followed. The majority of the people went to the upper floors of their dwellings and peered forth anxiously to catch sight of whatever might be roaming the streets waiting to devour them.

"If a lion is really at large it will certainly make things interesting," observed Snap. "But maybe it's only a scare."

"I hope it is," answered Giant. "Excuse me from brushing up against a real, bloodthirsty lion!" And he moved toward the Carson home, the others following.

"What is it, boys?" asked Shep's aunt, coming out on the piazza. "What is all the noise about?"

"They say a lion got loose from the circus," answered her nephew.

"Mercy on us!" ejaculated the lady, and turned pale. "Come in the house this minute, before you are all eat up!"

"We don't know if it is true or not," said Snap.

"Better not take any chances," answered Mrs. Carson. "I once heard of a lion getting loose from Central Park in New York City and eating up five school children."

"Yes, father tells that story, too," answered Shep. "But it was all a newspaper hoax—it never happened, aunty."

"Well, come in, and we'll close the doors and windows."

As much to please the lady as anything, the boys went in, and assisted in closing up the lower part of the house. They had just reached an upper window when a man went hurrying through the Street, holding a shotgun in his hands.

"Did a lion really get loose?" called out Snap.

"He certainly did," was the answer.

"Where is he now?"

"Somewhere back of the freight depot, or in one of the empty freight cars."

"Going to try to shoot him?" asked Whopper.

"Yes. Four or five of us are going to try to do that or capture him."

The man hurried on, and presently another appeared, armed with a rifle.

"Wish I had a gun; I'd go on the hunt, too," said Snap. "Think of laying a real lion low!"

"It would beat deer hunting, wouldn't it?" answered Whopper. "But supposing the lion turned and hunted you? You'd want to run about 'leven hundred miles!"

"If you had the chance," came from Giant. "I've heard that a lion can get over the ground as quick as a cat."

"I don't want any of you boys to leave this house until that lion is caught," said Mrs. Carson firmly. "I feel it my duty to keep you here."

"Maybe they won't catch him at all," suggested her nephew.

"Oh, they'll be sure to catch or shoot him by morning," answered the lady of the house.

Supper in the dining-room below was rather a haphazard affair. It was eaten behind closed blinds and in semi-darkness, the lady of the house being afraid to make a light, for fear of allowing the roaming lion to see the eating, and her guests. Just as the hired girl was bringing in the dessert a distant shot rang out, and uttering a scream the girl, whose nerves were on edge, let the dessert saucers fall to the floor with a crash.

"Somebody must have shot the lion!" cried Giant.

"Or shot at him," corrected Whopper.

"Just look what you have done, Mary!" cried Mrs. Carson in dismay.

"I couldn't help it, mum," answered the servant girl. "That lion gettin' loose has scared me stiff!"

"Well, I am scared myself. Clear up the muss, and be careful next time. Boys, you'll have to do without the preserves. But you can have cake."

"Cake is good enough for me," answered Snap, and the others said about the same.

Not long after that came another shot, this time from the corner at the end of the block.

"They are coming this way!" exclaimed the doctor's son. "Let us go upstairs again and see what is doing."

"Be careful!" screamed his aunt. "That lion may jump right up to the second story window!"

The boys went to an upper window, and then, growing bolder, stepped out on the top of the front piazza. They saw several men running along a cross street. Then another shot rang out.

"The lion must be in this vicinity," said Snap.

"I saw something then—over yonder!" cried Giant, and pointed to the back of a yard down by the corner of the street.

"A dog—and he is legging it for dear life," returned Whopper. "He looks as if he wouldn't stop this side of the North Pole!"

"Perhaps the lion scared him," said Shep. "I think—Look!"

The doctor's son broke off short and pointed with his hand. Gazing in the direction indicated, the lads saw something dark slinking on the opposite side of a high picket fence.

"It's the lion!" said Snap in a whisper. "See his tail swaying from side to side?"

"Oh, for a rifle!" murmured Whopper. "Aunty, have you a gun?" called Shep. "We see the lion!"

"No, I haven't any gun," answered the lady of the house quickly. "And you had better get inside as quickly as you can. The lion may leap up at you."

"I don't think he can jump so high."

"There are some of the men with their guns," went on Giant. "See, they are running around to the front of that house."

"I wonder if they see the lion?" asked Snap. "Let us yell to them," suggested Whopper. One after another the boys set up a shout. But the hunters were now out of sight and paid no attention to them.

A moment later the lads saw the lion leave the vicinity of the fence, cross the yard, and disappear behind the side of a barn. Then came a sudden smashing of boards, and a wild-eyed horse burst into view and ran down the street at top speed.

"The lion scared that horse," said Whopper. "Well, he's enough to scare anything."

"Boys! boys! why don't you come in?" pleaded Mrs. Carson. "If he sees you he'll surely try to get up on the piazza."

"If he turns this way we'll come in and shut the blinds," answered her nephew.

"It may be too late then."

"Oh, I think not, aunty."

Another shot rang out, and then the boys saw the men running around the barn.

"Perhaps they have managed to shut the lion in the barn,"

said Snap.

"If they are circus men they would rather capture the lion than kill him," returned the doctor's son. "Lions must be worth a good deal of money."

It was now about seven o'clock, and not as light as it had been. A few minutes passed and the men did not seem to be doing anything.

"Do you know what I think?" declared Whopper. "I think that lion is hiding on them."

"Just what I was going to say," came from Giant. "Maybe he has crawled to some dark corner of the barn and nobody has the courage to stir him up."

"Do you want to stir him up?" asked Snap dryly.

"Not on your necktie!" answered the small youth.

"Let him sleep in peace," added Whopper.

"He won't sleep," said the doctor's son.

"Something doing, now!" cried Whopper a few minutes later. He had seen one of the men run across the yard. "Why, I declare, there is the lion in the yard next door!"

"How did he get there?" asked Snap.

"I don't know."

"That man is going to take another shot!" cried Shep as he saw a gun raised.

"And there goes the lion!" cried Snap as the form of the animal arose swiftly in the air. With grace and precision the lord of the animal world cleared the back fence of the yard and crouched down in the street, close to a tree.

"He's heading this way!" burst out the doctor's son. "Maybe we had better get indoors."

"Oh, he can't leap up here," insisted Giant, who was brave, even though small.

"We'll take no chances," was Shep's answer. "Come."

He turned to the window, and so did Snap and Whopper. At that minute one of the men came around the corner of the street. The lion leaped from behind the tree into the roadway. Pulling up his gun, the man banged away wildly, for he was nervous and frightened.

"Oh!" came in a groan from Giant, and his chums saw him stagger.

"What is it?" asked Snap quickly. But instead of answering the small youth staggered around the piazza top.

"Giant is shot!" gasped Whopper. "Catch him! He is falling off the roof!"

Snap made a quick leap forward and caught Giant around the waist. Both were now on the slanting portion of the piazza roof. Snap did what he could to stay their progress, but it was in vain, and the next instant both boys slipped down over the edge. Snap clutched at a honeysuckle vine growing there, but it gave way, and a moment later the two boys rolled to the ground.

CHAPTER VI

SOMETHING ABOUT A CHIMPANZEE

It was well that that honeysuckle vine was growing there and that it gave way slowly after Snap grasped it, for otherwise the two boys might have suffered some broken bones. As it was, Snap bumped his shoulder severely and scraped his ear on the sand of the path that ran around the side of the house.

Poor Giant was unconscious, and even in that perilous moment Snap realized that his little chum had been hit by some of the shot from the gun. Whether the lad was dangerously wounded or not remained to be seen.

The two boys had fallen inside the dooryard, which was separated from the street by a low fence. Hardly did they land when Snap scrambled up, dragging Giant with him.

"The front door! The front door!" yelled Shep from above. "We'll let you in!" And then he leaped through the window and tore down the stairs four steps at a time, with Whopper at his heels.

As Snap turned and looked out into the street he saw a sight calculated to daunt the stoutest heart. The lion was there, standing erect, with bristling mane, glaring fiercely at him.

"Get away!" the boy yelled, not knowing what else to do. "Get away!" And then he picked up a whitewashed stone, one of a number bordering the garden path. With all his might he threw it at the lion and caught the beast in the head. The animal turned, slunk along the fence, and disappeared behind a tree in front of the next house.

The moment the animal turned away, Snap moved toward the piazza. He had Giant in one of his arms, and in his excitement did not notice the weight of his burden. As he ascended the steps the door was flung open and Shep appeared. Then Whopper showed himself, armed with an umbrella he had snatched from the hall rack.

"Where's the lion?" asked the doctor's son.

"Behind the tree!" gasped Snap, and then he literally fell into the hallway with Giant still in his arm. At once the door was closed and locked again.

"Was Giant shot?" queried Whopper, as he threw down the umbrella.

"Yes," answered Snap. "Make a light," he added, for the hallway was in total darkness.

Mrs. Carson was still upstairs, while the hired girl in her fright had fled to the garret, so the boys had to stumble around until Shep found a match and lit the lamp. Whopper and Snap carried Giant into the sitting-room and placed him on a sofa. As they did this the small youth opened his eyes and stared around wildly.

"The lion! Don't let him eat me!" he muttered.

"You're safe, Giant," answered the doctor's son.

"I—I got shot!"

"We know it. Let us see if you are badly hurt." On several occasions, in cases of accident, Shep had aided his father in caring for patients, and the knowledge thus gained now stood him in good stead. He made a close examination and found that several buckshot had grazed the small youth's temple, while one had gone through the tip of the ear. Giant's face was covered with blood, and this was washed off, and then his wounds were bathed with witch hazel and bound up.

"You had a narrow escape," was the comment of the doctor's son. "A little closer and you might have been killed, or might have lost your eyesight."

"That fellow with the gun was mighty careless," said Whopper.

"He was excited," added Snap. "He didn't want to hit Giant."

Snap said nothing about his hurt shoulder, although the bump he had received made him stiff and sore. He was thankful that the honeysuckle vine had broken the fall from the piazza roof, and that he and Giant had escaped from the clutches of the lion.

The hunters of the animal had gone past the house, and now those inside heard firing in the distance. The shots gradually grew fainter and fainter, at last dying out altogether.

"I guess his lionship has left town," said Shep.

"Or else he is dead," added Snap.

Mrs. Carson was much worried over the wounds Giant had received and insisted upon putting on them some salve. The boy declared he felt all right again and that the wounds would soon heal.

"I'm used to little things like that," he said. "When we went hunting we had all sorts of things happen to us."

"Mercy on us! Then you ought never to go hunting again!" declared the lady of the house.

"It was a narrow escape," said Snap gravely. "You can be thankful that man didn't blow your head off.

"I am thankful, Snap; and I am also thankful for what you did for me," murmured Giant, and looked at his chum in a manner that spoke volumes.

It was now too late to think of going to Fairview, for the last train had already departed. And as it was, Mrs. Carson insisted upon it that the boys remain all night.

"If you leave the house I'll be worried to death, thinking the lion caught you," she said.

So the boys stayed over another night. Late in the evening they stopped two men who were passing the house and from them learned that the lion had been chased to the edge of a big woods north of Railings. He had been wounded, of that the men were certain, and a regular hunting party was going out in the morning to either kill or capture the beast.

"The circus owner has offered a hundred dollars reward for his capture," said one of the men "So they'll get him alive if they can."

"Did any other lions escape?" asked the doctor's son.

"No; but one of the big monkeys is missing—the educated one."

"Do you mean Abe, the educated chimpanzee?" queried Snap.

"That's the fellow—the one who eats, drinks, smokes and does all sorts of stunts. He's missing, and the circus men are more worried over him than over the lion. One man said the chim— what-do-you-call-him was worth a thousand dollars."

"I believe that—being educated to do so many things," said Whopper. "He sat up to a table to eat just like a man."

"Did you hear how the lion and the chimpanzee happened to get away?" asked Giant.

"Why, there was a report it was the fault of four rascals who used to work for the circus—three men who were discharged for getting drunk, and a boy who did stunts on the trapeze and ran away."

"That boy!" cried Snap. "Oh, I don't think he had anything to do with it."

"Well, that's what the circus men say. If they catch the men and the boy they'll have the whole crowd locked up."

"I am sure the boy is innocent," said the doctor's son.

"I got shot by somebody hunting that lion," said Giant. "Do you know who fired his shotgun out yonder?"

"Oh, that was Hank Donaldson. He's always blowing about what he can do with a gun, and he was so worked up and nervous he killed Mack's dog and smashed the plate-glass window in the new five-and-ten-cent store. He got scared to death when somebody told him a boy over here fell from the roof and got hit. Is it bad?"

"No, but it might have been."

"You ought to pitch into Hank. He ought to know better than to fire so promiscuous-like in the city streets. He meant well, but if he had killed you, what then?" And the man passed on, shaking his head earnestly.

In the morning Giant felt quite like himself and insisted upon leaving off the bandage that had been placed over his forehead.

"I don't want to become an object of curiosity," he explained. "Even as it is, I suppose lots of folks will want to know all about it."

While the boys were eating the door bell rang, and the hired girl announced a man to see the lad who had been shot. The visitor proved to be Hank Donaldson, a big, burly fellow, now nervous to the degree of collapsing.

"I—I hope yer don't think I did it a-purpose," said Donaldson. "'Cos I didn't—I only wanted to shoot that 'ere lion, 'fore he ate sombuddy up."

"I understand," answered Giant. "But you were very careless. After this you had better give up lion hunting."

"I sure will. I am very sorry—yes, I am. Hope you'll forgive it."

"I will—if you didn't mean it," answered Giant.

"I've got a heap o' troubles, I have," went on Hank Donaldson. "Got to pay 'bout a hundred dollars fer a plate-glass winder I smashed, an' got to pay fer a dorg, too. Ye don't catch me huntin' lions no more." And he heaved a mountainous sigh. A few minutes later he departed, saying he hoped Giant would soon get over his hurts.

"I guess he will be punished enough when he pays for the glass and the dog," said the small youth, and smiled in spite of his wounds.

Getting a ladder, the boys fixed up the brokendown honeysuckle vine, and then bid good-by to Mrs. Carson. She was still a bit timid about letting them go.

"You keep your eyes open for that lion," she said. "And if you see him, run into the first house or store that's handy. Don't think you can shoo him off again with a stone, because it isn't likely you'll be able to."

"We'll be on our guard, aunty," answered Shep.

The circus had left town, as it was billed to perform in another city forty miles away. But several employees had been left behind, and these men, aided by a number of others, went on a long hunt for the lion and the chimpanzee. The lion had been seen making for the woods, but what had become of the chimpanzee nobody knew.

"The loss of that chimpanzee is a big one for the circus," said Snap, while on the way home. "Just see how they feature him on the bills. They have other lions, but Abe was their only man-monkey."

What the youth said about the chimpanzee was true. Abe, as he had been named, was a wonderful drawing-card. At first a reward of fifty dollars was offered for his return, and later this sum was increased. It may be as well to state here that the owner of the circus suspected that the men who had been discharged by him had the chimpanzee and would have it returned to him when the reward was large enough. What had become of the men nobody knew, and the boy acrobat had likewise disappeared.

"That boy interested me," said Snap. "I'd like to meet him again and have a talk with him."

"Maybe we will meet him again some time," answered the doctor's son.

"Oh, it's not likely. There won't be anything to keep him in these parts. If he is a regular acrobat, more than likely he'll join some other circus or some vaudeville show."

"He didn't look as if he liked the life," said Whopper.

"That's the way it struck me," came from Giant.

When the boys got home they had quite a story to tell. Mrs. Caslette was much alarmed over the injuries her son had received and insisted upon it that Giant let Dr. Reed attend him, which the physician did willingly.

"Not much damaged," said the doctor. "But he had what folks call a close shave."

The boys told the doctor about what they had learned from Mr. Jally, and in turn he gave them instructions concerning the photographs he desired them to obtain during their outing in the Windy Mountains. As there might be a little delay in getting the new cameras and in getting some other supplies the start of the trip was postponed until Tuesday.

"And how do you propose to go?" asked Snap of the doctor's son.

"Father thinks it would be wise for us to row to Firefly Lake. Then we can hide our boat and tote our supplies over to the mountains."

"That suits me, Shep."

"Did Ham Spink and his crowd go that way?" asked Whopper.

"I think they did, but I am not sure."

"Well, I don't want to meet them if they did," came from Giant. "They can keep their distance and we'll keep ours."

CHAPTER VII

UP THE RIVER

Coming from Sunday-school on Sunday afternoon the boys fell in with Jed Sanborn, the old hunter who had gone out with them on more than one trip. They were rather surprised to see the man carrying his shotgun, for Jed usually believed in respecting the Sabbath day.

"Been out hunting?" queried Snap as all came to a halt.

"Well, yes, kind of," answered the old hunter. "But not any reg'lar game."

"I didn't think you'd be out on Sunday," said Whopper.

"I took it into my head yesterday to look fer that lion as got away at Railings," was Jed Sanborn's answer. "Somebuddy said as how he was keepin' shady over to Merrick's woods, so I tramped over. Stayed in the woods all night an' this mornin'."

"Did you see the lion?" asked Snap eagerly.

"Nary a hair o' him, lad, an' I don't think he's in the woods, nuther."

"But he must be somewhere," insisted Giant.

"Thet might be, but he ain't in Merrick's woods. I'll bet a glass o' cider on't." Jed Sanborn looked at the boys and grinned. "Goin' out huntin' ag'in, so I hear."

"Yes."

"Whereabouts this time—up whar ye see the ghost?" And the old man chuckled, thinking of what the ghost had proved to be.

"No. We are going over to Windy Mountains this trip," answered the doctor's son.

"That far, eh? It's quite a trip. Hope ye find it wuth so long a journey. I don't know as the game thar is any better nor around the lakes close to hum."

"We are going for the fun of camping partly," said Shep. He did not care to say anything about the picture-taking for his father. "Do you expect to come out that way?"

"I might."

"If you do you must hunt us up," put in Snap.

"I'll do thet, sure pop," answered Jed Sanborn. He started off, then turned back. "Oh, I say!" he called.

"What is it?" asked Whopper.

"It's about thet pesky Ham Spink," went on the old hunter. "Did I tell ye about my spring?"

"No. What of it?" asked Giant.

"Ye know I've got a nice spring o' cold water up by my cabin. Well, some days ago Ham Spink an' thet Dudder boy came up there, an' on the sly caved the spring in on me. I caught 'em coming away. I had my shotgun with me, an' I was mad, good an' proper. I said they must fix the spring or somebuddy'd git shot. They got scart, I kin tell ye, an' they got on their hands an' knees in the sand an' rocks an' mud and worked like beavers till they had the spring fixed. It jest about ruined their clothes, an' when they went off they was as mad as hops. Spink said he would square up, but he's a blower an' I ain't afraid o' him."

"It was just like Ham's meanness, and Carl Dudder's meanness, too," said Snap.

The new cameras and supplies had come in on Saturday night, and on Monday morning the boys received a new tent from Dr. Reed, and a tarpaulin from Mr. Dodge. Mr. Dawson gave the boys some blankets, and Mrs. Caslette promised to supply them with a hamper of table delicacies.

"With so many good things we'll have a better time than ever before," said Snap.

"Nothing like winding up the summer in good shape," answered the doctor's son.

The chums went over their boat with care, to make certain that it did not leak, and then looked over their guns and the rest of their outfit. On Monday evening everything was taken down to the boathouse for readiness early Tuesday morning.

"I am glad of one thing," remarked Whopper. "Ham Spink and his crowd are not on hand to molest our things, as they tried to do before."

"Well, we gave 'em a warm reception when they did come to the boathouse," answered Snap with a grin, referring to an event related in detail in "*The Young Hunters of the Lake.*"

For this particular outing the supplies were extra numerous, and the boys knew it was going to be no light task to transport them by boat and pack.

"We'll have to make the best of it," said the doctor's son. "When we are in the boat we'll have to row with care, and if we can't tote the stuff over to the mountains in one trip we'll make two."

It was somewhat gloomy Monday evening, and the boys were fearful that it might rain by morning. But the clouds cleared away during the night and the sun came up in the morning as brightly as ever. Each got an early breakfast, and by eight o'clock all were assembled at the boathouse.

"Everything all right?" asked Whopper, who was the last to arrive.

"All O.K.," answered Snap.

Soon the supplies were stowed away with care, and then the chums entered the craft. It was agreed that two should row at a time, and Snap and Giant took up the oars. Several men and boys had gathered to see them start.

"Don't forget to bring back another bear!" sang out one man.

"If you should happen to see that lion, better run for it," cautioned another.

"We don't expect to see the lion, and we aren't looking for more bears," answered Snap. "We are going to take it easy this trip."

"Well, I wish you luck," said the man. Then the boys set up a cheer from the shore, and the chums answered it.

"Say, Snap, what makes you think this is going to be a real quiet picnic?" asked Whopper on the way. "Now, I expect to bag about fifty rabbits, a hundred partridges, some wild turkeys, a bear or two, and that lion in the bargain!"

"Wow!" gasped Giant. "Whopper is to the front once more.

Why not make it two lions while you are at it?"

"Because there is only one, and I don't want to be—er—piggish."

"Why not say lionish?" questioned Shep.

"Aren't you going to hunt at all?" demanded the boy who loved to exaggerate.

"Of course," drawled Giant. "I am going to hunt ants, and June bugs, and horseflies, and worms, and—"

"Oh, come off!" growled Whopper. "You know what I mean."

"To be sure we'll hunt," said the doctor's son. "But the cameras are going ahead of the guns this trip."

"Speaking of cameras and worms puts me in mind of something I heard yesterday," said Snap. "It's about trick photography. An amateur photographer showed a picture he had of what looked like a fierce snake on a rail fence. By and by he gave the trick away. The snake was nothing but a garden worm wound around some little sticks and toothpicks, and the picture had been snapped at close range."

"That's like a trick picture I heard about, taken on two plates," said Giant. "It was one of a man wheeling himself in a wheelbarrow."

"I know of three fellows who took a queer-looking picture," said Whopper. "Now, this is true," he continued, noticing the others look of doubt. "They got an oilcloth sign, a square one, and then one fellow got up on another fellow's shoulders. The two fellows held the sign in front of them while the third chap took the picture. When the photo was printed it looked as if the boy carrying the sign was about nine feet high."

"I heard of that in a different way," said Snap. "A fellow out in the country took two horses back of a henhouse. He had the head of one horse sticking beyond one end of the henhouse and the hind legs of the second horse sticking out at the other end, and the picture looked as if that horse was fifteen or twenty feet long."

On they went along the river, past Pop Lundy's orchard, where they had once had quite an adventure. It was rather warm, but a light breeze cooled those at the oars. Snap and Giant rowed for about a mile and were then relieved by their chums, and thus they changed about until it was time for lunch, when they ran ashore at an inviting spot.

"Rowing makes a fellow hungry," observed Whopper. "I think I can eat at least fifteen sandwiches, not to mention some cake and a few pieces of pie."

"Perhaps you want the whole lunch yourself," said Snap. "Well, you don't get it."

"Anybody want coffee?" asked Shep. "If so we'll have to start up a fire."

"Don't bother to-day. Water is good enough," said Giant, and so they rested in the shade of the trees and ate their sandwiches and a pie Mrs. Caslette had baked for them, washing the food down with water from a handy spring.

"I am going to take my first picture," said Snap, and made the others get in a group, each with a piece of pie in his hand. He took a snapshots and then marked the picture in a book he had brought along for that purpose.

"What do you call it?" asked Whopper.

"Pie-ous Time," answered Snap, and then dodged a tin cup the other flung at him.

"We must try to reach Lake Cameron before night," said Shep, when they were once more on the way. "I shouldn't care to camp out along the river."

"Oh, you might find a worse spot," answered Snap. "However, we'll get to the lake if we can."

As my old readers know, Lake Cameron was connected with the river by a narrow creek, the banks of which were overhung with bushes. Since the boys had come home from their last outing the rains had been heavy, consequently the creek was well filled with water.

"This makes getting through easy, and I am glad of it," said Whopper. "I was afraid we'd have to carry some of the stuff around, so as to lighten the boat."

"Are you going up the lake shore very far tonight?" questioned Giant. It was already growing dark.

"No, I think we had best camp near the mouth of the creek," answered the doctor's son, and the others agreed with him.

As soon as the lake was reached Giant, who was the best fisherman of the crowd, baited up and threw out his line. For some time he did not get a bite, but then came a sharp tug, so dear to the heart of the angler.

"What have you got?" asked Whopper.

"Might be an elephant, but I—I guess not," cried the small youth.

The others stopped rowing and Giant began to play his catch with care. Soon he brought to light a fine pickerel, and dropped the fish in the bottom of the boat.

"Good for Giant!" cried Snap. "A couple of more like that and we'll have a dandy fish supper."

Again the line was baited and thrown in and the boys took up their rowing. Presently came another tug and again Giant was successful, bringing in a fish several inches larger than the first.

"This is pickerel day," cried Whopper "Reckon I'll try my luck," and he did, and presently brought in a pickerel almost as large as the others. But that was the end of the luck for the time being.

"Never mind," said Shep. "Three are enough. Now to land and get our camp into shape for the night—and then for supper." And a few minutes later a landing was made.

CHAPTER VIII

THE FIRST NIGHT OUT

The boys knew the shores of Lake Cameron well, having camped there before, and they selected a spot that just suited their wants. The rowboat was drawn up in a tiny cove and made fast, and then all hands set to work getting the tent and some of the outfit ashore. The things left in the boat were covered carefully with the tarpaulin, to keep off the night dampness and a possible rain.

Shep had been selected as the leader during this outing, on account of what his father had done for the club, and he now directed Giant and Whopper to build the fire and get supper ready, while he and Snap erected the tent and cut some pine boughs for bedding.

"It will be almost warm enough to-night to sleep out of doors," said the doctor's son. "But it seems more natural to sleep under some kind of a cover."

He and Snap took the ax and soon cut down three slender saplings and trimmed them. Two were planted in the ground where the tent was to be erected and the third was laid across the top, in little limb-crotches left for that purpose. Then the canvas was thrown over and pegged down tightly, sides and back. The front of the tent had a double flap, which could be tied shut with strings if desired.

Long before the tent was up and furnished with bedding of pine boughs, Giant and Whopper had the camp fire started, and soon an appetizing odor of coffee and frying fish filled the air. It was now quite dark, and the glare of the fire made the scene a pleasant one.

"Camping wouldn't be camping without a fire," observed Snap, as, having finished his share of the work, he sat down on a grassy hillock to rest and watch Giant and Whopper getting ready to serve the evening meal.

"Right you are, Snap," answered Shep. "Even in the hottest of weather I love to see the glare and the flickering shadows."

"I always think of good stories and plenty to eat when I see a camp fire," came from Giant.

"Well, I reckon we are going to have the eating, even if we don't have the stories," said the doctor's son.

"What's the matter with Whopper spinning one of his outrageous yarns?" suggested Snap. "He must be fairly aching to tell something marvelous."

"I tell only truthful tales," came from the storyteller modestly. "Now, if you want to hear—"

"Truthful tales!" burst out Giant. "Say, Whopper, that's the very biggest whopper you ever told!"

"All right, then, I won't tell any stories," returned the other lad reproachfully.

"Oh, yes, you will; you can't help it," said Snap.

Supper was soon served. It consisted of bread and butter and coffee and pickerel done to a turn, topped off with some crullers from a bagful donated by Mrs. Caslette. The boys took their time eating, and when they had finished the bones of the fish were picked clean. Then Giant said something about a train falling off a bridge, and that started Whopper to telling a most marvelous story of an engineer who, seeing that a bridge was down, put on all speed and rushed his train over a gap thirty feet wide in safety. The others listened with sober faces until Whopper had finished, and then burst out laughing.

"What did I tell you?" cried Snap. "I said Whopper couldn't help telling a yarn."

"And such a one, too!" added Giant.

"And of course we all believe it," came from the doctor's son.

"Well, I had to do something—to help pass the time," said Whopper a bit sheepishly.

"Sure you did," said Snap heartily. "It's all right, Whopper— only don't ask us to believe such a story."

"Is anybody going to stand guard to-night?" asked Giant to change the subject.

"What's the use?" questioned Snap. "I don't think anybody or anything will come to disturb us."

"Well, you can never tell," said Shep slowly. "But if you fellows don't care to stand guard we'll let it go at that."

"Oh, it's for you to say, Shep—you are leader this trip."

"Well, I guess we can all turn in."

And turn in they did about nine o'clock, with the understanding that they were to have breakfast at six in the morning and continue their journey as soon after that as possible.

Whether he felt the responsibility of leadership or not it would be hard to say, but certain it is that the doctor's son did not sleep near as soundly as did the others. He was very restless, and when he dozed off it was to dream of the lion that had escaped from the circus. He imagined that the animal had followed them to their camp and was bending over him and licking his face. He uttered a groan of terror and sat up and opened his eyes. As he did this a dark form leaped over him and out of the open tent. The fire had burned low, so what the form was Shep could not tell.

"Help!" screamed the doctor's son. He was not yet fully awake.

"Wha—what's the matter?" spluttered Snap, throwing aside his blanket.

"What's wrong?" came from Whopper and Giant simultaneously.

"Something—a wild animal—in here—jumped over me!" gasped Shep. "It just went outside!"

"Oh, you are dreaming, Shep," said Snap.

"No, I'm not. I saw it—felt it! Let me get my gun!"

The doctor's son threw off his blanket, leaped up and grasped his shotgun, that hung on one of the tent poles. He stepped to the opening of the tent and peered out anxiously.

"See anything?" demanded Whopper. He and the others were now up, and each was arming himself.

"N—no."

"I told you you were dreaming," came from Snap.

"Too many crullers for supper," was Giant's comment. "Sometimes they lay like lead in a fellow's stomach and give him all sorts of dreams."

"It wasn't the crullers," persisted the doctor's son. "I'm going outside and investigate." And he stepped out in the direction of the camp fire.

"Be careful," warned Snap. "If any wild beasts are around you want to be on your guard."

The doctor's son looked around with care, but could see no trace of the night visitor. He stirred up the camp fire and soon had a bright blaze going. The others had followed him outside and they stood shivering in the damp air.

"False alarm, I guess," said Giant, yawning. "What time is it?"

"One o'clock," answered Whopper, after consulting his watch. "Say, this is a dandy way of breaking up one's rest," he added sarcastically.

"If you don't believe I saw something—and felt something— you needn't," returned Shep tartly.

"Must have been a sand flea, or a water bug."

"Come, Whopper, don't get mad," came from Snap. "If Shep—"

"There it is, behind the bushes!" burst out the doctor's son. "I just saw its eyes shining!"

As he spoke he raised his shotgun. But the eyes had disappeared.

"I saw something," came from Giant. "See, it's moving—back of the huckleberry bush."

Something was moving, that was evident, but what it was none of the young hunters could make out. Shep raised his gun again.

"Shall I take a chance and fire?" he asked of the others.

"Might as well," answered Whopper. "It couldn't be anything but a wild animal."

"Wait," cried Snap. He raised his voice. "Who is there?" he called out. "Answer, or we'll shoot!"

For reply there came a sound that thoroughly astonished the boys. It was the bark of a dog, low and uncertain. Then there stepped into view a collie, wagging his tail doubtfully.

"A dog!" cried Giant. "Come here! come here!" he called, and gave an inviting whistle.

Slowly the dog came forward, still wagging his tail doubtfully. When he was quite close he sat up on his haunches and began to move his fore paws up and down.

"He's begging!" cried Snap. "He must be hungry."

"I suppose he smelled our food and came for some," said Giant. "Good little dog!" he cried. "Come here!" And as he snapped his fingers the collie came up to him and allowed the small youth to pat him on the head.

"That's your wild beast, Shep," said Whopper.

"Well, I knew it was something," answered the doctor's son. "That dog must have been in the tent."

"More than likely," answered Snap. "See how friendly he is," he added, for the collie was now leaping from one to another of the boys and barking joyfully. Giant gave him a cruller and he ate the dainty greedily.

"He's half starved," said Snap. "Must have wandered off into the woods and got lost."

"Is there a name on his collar?" asked Whopper.

"No, only a license number," answered Giant after an examination. "Looks to me as if he might be a valuable animal."

"I think I've seen that collie before," said Shep.

"So you did—in the tent," said Whopper quickly, and set up a laugh.

"Oh, you know what I mean. He has a regular star on his breast. Yes, I am sure I've seen him somewhere, but where I can't remember."

"He ought to be returned to his owner," said Snap. "But how we are going to do it I don't know. I don't care to go back just for the dog."

"Nor I," added Giant. "Let us take him along and bring him back with us when we come."

"If he'll stay with us," came from Whopper. "He may—if we feed him well," answered the doctor's son.

They let the dog have another cruller and the heads of the fish, and the animal made a meal of them. The boys felt cold and tired and crawled back into the tent to finish their night's rest. Soon the collie came nosing at the opening.

"Come here!" said Giant in a low voice, and instantly the dog nestled down at his side, and there he remained until daylight.

"We can take him in some of our pictures," said the small youth. "He'll add to the picturesqueness."

"What are you going to call him?" asked Whopper.

"Sphinx."

"And why Sphinx?" asked Snap.

"Because he won't tell us who he is, where he came from, or anything about himself."

"Oh, that's not a pretty name," cried the doctor's son. "I vote we call him Wags, because he wags his tail so much."

"All right, Wags it is," said Giant. "What do you say, Wags?" he added, turning to the dog.

The collie barked and wagged his tail vigorously. Evidently he was perfectly satisfied.

As the lads had no more game or fish to eat, they made a hasty meal of bacon, bread, crullers and coffee. As soon as the repast was over they took down the tent and placed that and the other things on board the rowboat. The collie had been fed and was more frisky than ever.

"Wonder if he'll go into the boat with us?" said Snap. "Some dogs don't like the water."

"Most collies do," answered Giant. "I'll try him." He called Wags, and the dog leaped into the craft and took his place at the bow.

"He'll do for a lookout," said Whopper. "Come on, it's time to start."

They looked around the temporary camp, to make certain that nothing had been left behind, then entered the rowboat and shoved off. Snap and Whopper took the oars, and soon they were on the journey up Lake Cameron to Firefly Lake.

"Don't forget one thing," said Snap shortly after starting. "If possible we want to bring down some sort of game for dinner. It won't do to use up our canned things and that stuff."

"Everybody watch out," said Giant. "And if we can't shoot something, why, toward dinner time, I'll try my hand at fishing again."

CHAPTER IX

INTO THE RAPIDS

It was another ideal day, and the young hunters felt in the best of spirits. Whopper felt so good that presently he burst out singing an old school song, and the others joined in.

"That's all right, and very good, but if we want any game we've got to keep quiet," said the doctor's son after the song was ended.

"Right you are," answered Whopper promptly. "And as I'd rather eat later than sing now I'll shut up."

They followed the shore line of Lake Cameron, heading for the rocky watercourse that connected that body of water with Firefly Lake. The eyes of all were on the alert for game, and toward the middle of the forenoon Giant called a halt.

"I saw something in the trees yonder," he said, pointing ashore. "Looked to me as if they might be partridge."

"Partridge would suit me first rate," answered Snap. "Let us land and try our luck."

"Making as little noise as possible they beached the rowboat and Giant silenced the dog, not knowing what he might do while on a hunt.

Captain Ralph Bonehill

"Perhaps he's a good bird dog and perhaps he isn't," he said. "We'll take no chances."

Each of the young hunters had his shotgun, and one after another they followed Shep to the spot where the game had been seen among the trees. High among the branches of a silver maple tree they saw some ruffed grouse, commonly known to many sportsmen as partridge.

"There's our chance," said the doctor's son. "Who is to fire?"

"Let us all take a chance," pleaded Giant. "Just to open the outing, you know."

Shep was willing, and said he would give the word. With great caution they crept as close as possible to the grouse. The birds were on three branches of the maple, one over the other.

Silently the four boy hunters raised their firearms. Shep looked at them and then along the barrel of his piece.

"Fire!" said he, and one shot rang out after another quickly. There was a mad whirring and fluttering from the ruffed grouse. Two dropped like lead, while two others flew around in a circle, badly wounded. Then the boys discharged their guns again, and wounded two more birds. As the game came down they rushed in and wrung the necks of those not already dead.

"Six, all told," said Giant proudly. "That's one and a half apiece."

"Not so bad," answered Snap.

"It's dandy!" shouted Whopper, throwing up his cap in his delight. "Now we can have roast partridge for dinner, and supper, too, if we want to."

"Right you are," came from Shep. "I believe we all made a hit," he added.

"A hit?" repeated Whopper. "We all made home runs!" And at this reference to baseball all of the boys laughed.

Taking the game to the rowboat, they resumed their journey, and by noon reached the watercourse connecting the two lakes. Here they stopped at a spot well known to them and built a camp fire, and here they roasted all of the game, fearing it might not keep in such hot weather.

"I'm going to try baking 'em in mud," said Giant, who had learned the trick from Jed Sanborn. Leaving the feathers on the grouse the lad plastered each bird thickly with some clayey mud, and then placed them in the fire to roast, or bake, as he called it. He watched them with care and tried one frequently to see if it was done.

"Now I guess this will do," he said at last, and cracked the baked mud from the grouse. With the mud came the feathers of the bird, leaving the meat clean. The grouse was tender and juicy and done to a turn.

"Giant, you'll have to get a job as a chef in a big hotel," said the doctor's son, smacking his lips over the feast. "This game certainly couldn't be, better."

"Why not leave some of the partridge right in the baked mud?" suggested Snap. "It ought to keep well that way."

"We can try it," said Whopper.

The collie was given his share of the dinner and appeared to enjoy it as much as the boys. He acted as if he felt perfectly at home with the young hunters, and made no offer to leave them.

"If he wasn't such a fine dog I'd put him down as an outcast," said Shep. "But nobody would abandon such a fine animal—

he's worth too much money."

Once again the boy hunters proceeded on their way. As they entered the watercourse connecting the two lakes they noticed that the current was flowing swiftly.

"The heavy rains are responsible for this," said Snap. "We want to be careful, or the boat will be smashed on some of the rocks."

"We might get out and walk—that is, some of us—if the shore wasn't so rough and rocky," said Whopper. "It looks wilder than ever now, doesn't it, boys?"

It certainly did look wilder—or was it only the rushing of the water that made it appear so? They rowed on with caution, two at the oars and two doing the steering with poles. Wags sat in the bow as before, watching proceedings in silence.

About half the distance to Firefly Lake had been covered when they came to a sharp turn in the watercourse. Here the water boiled and foamed around several sharp rocks.

"Beware of the rocks!" sang out the doctor's Son.

"To the right! To the right!" yelled Whopper. "It's too shallow on the other side!"

They tried to turn the craft to the right, but the current seemed too strong for them. The boat swung around and hit one of the rocks a sharp blow. There was a little splash as the collie went overboard. Then came a big souse, that covered those who remained in the boat with spray.

"Giant is overboard!" cried Whopper. "And so is the dog!"

"Let the dog take care of himself," cried Snap. "Grab Giant!"

Whopper turned to catch the lad who had gone overboard, but

the current was too quick for him, and the small youth was sent whirling out of his reach.

For the moment it looked as if the rowboat would either go over or be stove in on the rocks, and those left on board had to turn their attention to the craft. They saw Giant floundering in the boiling water, but could do nothing to aid him.

"Swing her around and pull for shore; it's our only chance!" cried Snap. "Quick, now—or we'll all go to the bottom!"

Fighting desperately, the three lads swung the craft around slowly. It scraped on more of the rocks, and one of the oars was caught and snapped off like a pipe-stem. But then the boat struck water that was a little more calm, and soon they reached a cove and felt themselves safe for the time being.

"Where is Giant?" was Shep's question as soon as they knew the outfit was secure.

"There he is, on one of the rocks," answered Whopper. "And here comes the dog," he added as the collie came battling bravely toward them.

Soon Wags was on shore and shaking himself vigorously, acting as if such a bath was a daily occurrence.

"Hello, you fellows!" came in Giant's voice. He was sprawled out on a rock in midstream, sixty feet away.

"Are you hurt?" questioned Shep anxiously.

"No; the water was pretty soft," answered the small youth. "But I say, how am I going to get ashore?"

"Can't you wade it?" asked Whopper.

"No; don't try that—the current is too swift," cried Snap.

"Well, we can't take the boat to him," said Whopper.

"I know that."

"We might throw him a line," suggested the doctor's son.

"Yes, that's an idea."

A light but strong line was brought forth and Shep curled it up as a cowboy does a lasso. Then he made a cast, but the line fell short.

"Let me try it," said Snap.

One after another the boys on shore tried to reach Giant with the line but failed. After Whopper had made his cast Wags, who had been sitting on a rock watching proceedings with interest, gave a bark and caught the end of the line in his teeth.

"There's an idea!" cried Snap. "Let the dog carry the line."

"Will he do it?" questioned Whopper.

"We can try him and see."

The end of the line was made fast to the collie's collar, and Giant was told to call him.

"Come, Wags! That's a good dog! Come!" called the small youth, and whistled and snapped his fingers.

At first Wags appeared to be doubtful, but finally he ventured into the water. Then he began to swim steadily toward the rock, dragging the line behind him.

"What a shame if the current carries him away!" murmured Whopper.

"We'll not allow that," answered the doctor's son. "If he loses ground we can haul him in."

Slowly but surely the dog drew closer to the rock. At last he got within Giant's reach, and the youth caught him and pulled him up.

"Tie the rope about your waist and we'll haul you to shore!" sang out Shep. "Bring the dog on your shoulder if you can."

"I'll try it," answered Giant.

It was no easy matter for him, on the wet and slippery rock, to adjust the rope and get the collie on his shoulder. But presently he announced that he was ready, and the boys on shore commenced to haul in. Down in the madly rushing water went Giant, and it was all he could do to keep his feet. But luck was with him, and in a very few minutes he and the dog were safe.

"That was quite an adventure," he said when he had recovered his breath.

"You went overboard in a great hurry," remarked Whopper. "And so did Wags."

"The shock to the boat did it. It made me lose my balance before I was aware."

"Let us be thankful Giant is safe, and Wags," said the doctor's son. "And thankful, too, that the boat didn't go over. If it had our outing would have been spoiled."

"We've got to be mighty careful how we travel through the rest of this river," remarked Snap. "The heavy rains have made a fierce torrent of it."

It must be confessed that the boys did not know exactly what to do. Should they venture on the river again, or carry the outfit to the beginning of Firefly Lake?

"I've got an idea," said Shep at last. "You can follow it or not, as you think best. My idea is to have two of the crowd take the boat down and the two others walk to Firefly Lake, carrying the most precious of the outfit."

"That suits me," said Snap.

"Who will walk and who take the boat?" questioned Whopper.

"I might as well go in the boat—I'm wet already," said Giant, smiling grimly.

"The three of us can draw lots as to who shall go with Giant," said the doctor's son.

The drawing was at once made, and it fell to Snap to go with the small youth. The cameras and guns were taken from the rowboat and also a few other things. Then the doctor's son and Whopper aided the others in getting the boat into the rushing river once more.

"Take care of yourselves!" cried Shep. "If all goes right you'll get to the lake long before we do."

In a moment the boat was caught by the current and whirled onward. Giant and Snap had all they could do to steer it. But, fortunately, they found no more such bad places as those already encountered, and in less than an hour found themselves floating on Firefly Lake, safe and sound.

"The others might have come with us after all," declared Giant. "Wonder how long it will take them to reach here?"

"I don't know; it depends on how rough they find the way. Maybe a couple of hours," answered Snap. "We may as well go ashore, start up a camp and wait for them."

CHAPTER X

THE CABIN IN THE WOODS

The doctor's son and Whopper had no easy time of it making their way through the bushes and around the rocks which lined the watercourse between the two lakes. There was no trail on that side of the stream, and they had to "go it blind," to use Shep's words.

"Say, this is worse than climbing a mountain!" gasped Whopper, after slipping and sliding over a number of rocks and coming down rather suddenly in a hollow.

"Rather knocks the breath out of a fellow," returned Shep. "Take care that you don't sprain an ankle, Whopper."

"That's what I'm watching out for. I don't want my whole outing spoiled."

After a large amount of hard walking and climbing they managed to cover about half the distance to Firefly Lake. But by that time both were so exhausted the doctor's son called a halt.

"No use of killing ourselves," he said. "We can't go any farther than the lake to-day, anyway."

"Hope Snap and Giant wait for us at the mouth of the river," said Whopper. "I don't want to tramp along the lake

Captain Ralph Bonehill

shore afoot."

"Oh, they'll wait, and mostly likely start a camp."

"Say, if I remember rightly the river makes a bend to the right here," went on Whopper after a pause. "And if that is so, what's the matter with our striking inland a short distance and cutting off some of the walk?"

"I'm willing—anything to reach Firefly Lake before it gets too dark to see."

Having rested themselves, the boys commenced to draw away from the river shore, taking to the woods, where the walking was easier. It was now close to six o'clock, and the sun was going down over the trees to the westward.

"Hope they have supper ready by the time we get there," said Whopper after a period of silence. "This transit is making me as hungry as a bear."

"Same here. Well, we'll have the partridge to fall back on, even if they don't cook anything else."

The two young hunters tramped on. As they walked they kept their eyes open for a possible sight of game. So far all they had seen were some birds, not worth shooting.

Another quarter of a mile was covered when they came to a patch of spruces. As they advanced they saw several rabbits leap from beside one of the trees.

"A chance for a shot!" cried the doctor's son, and speedily swung his shotgun into position, an example followed by his chum. Both young hunters blazed away without delay, and each was successful in laying a rabbit low. Before they could fire again the rest of the game was out of sight.

"Not very large," was Shep's comment as they picked up the

game. "But the rabbits are young, and they'll make fine eating."

"It is a good thing that new game law isn't in effect yet," said Whopper. "If it was we'd not be allowed to shoot rabbits until next October."

"You are right, Whopper—hunting will be a good deal more restricted after the new laws go into effect."

Placing the rabbits in a gamebag, the two chums walked on, past the clump of spruces and then across a little clearing. Here, much to their surprise, they came in sight of a dilapidated cabin. It was a small affair of rough logs with a rude stone chimney and one window and one door. One end of the cabin sagged greatly, as if on the point of falling down.

"I hadn't any idea this was here," was the comment of the doctor's son. "Wonder who it can belong to?"

"Perhaps some hunters put it up in days gone by," returned Whopper. "It doesn't look as if it was inhabited."

"Let's go in and take a look around," suggested Shep. It was his delight to poke around in new and odd places.

"We don't want to lose time," was his chum's reply. "It will be dark before you know it."

"Oh, it won't take long to look," answered Shep.

The old cabin was surrounded by weeds and bushes, and they had to fairly work their way to the doorway.

"Somebody has been here, that's certain," cried the doctor's son. "Here are eggshells and newly picked chicken feathers."

"Hello, in there!" cried Whopper, poking his head into the small doorway. He could not see, for the cabin inside was dark.

Scarcely had the word been uttered when a most surprising thing happened. Something whizzed through the air, directly between the heads of the two boy hunters. It was a good-sized chunk of wood, and it struck a rock outside with a thud.

"Why—why—stop that!" stammered Whopper, and fell back, and Shep did the same.

"Evidently somebody doesn't want visitors," was the comment of the doctor's son. "I say," he called out, "what do you mean by heaving that wo—"

Crash! From the interior of the cabin came another chunk of wood, a gnarled root, just grazing Shep's shoulder. Then a stone followed, striking Whopper a glancing blow on the hip. Both lads retreated in confusion.

"Well, of all things!" gasped the doctor's son when he could get his breath. "That's a cordial welcome, I must say."

"Have you any idea who it was?"

"Not the slightest. It was too dark to see anybody."

"Couldn't be any of the Ham Spink crowd?"

"No. I don't think they'd treat us in just that way."

"Maybe it's some crazy chap."

"That's more like it—some hermit like old Peter Peterson," returned Shep, referring to an old man who lived near the lakes and who rarely showed himself in any of the settlements.

"Peter Peterson wasn't crazy; he didn't heave things at folks."

"Let us see if we can get him to come out. I'd like to see what sort of a chap he is."

Keeping at what they thought was a safe distance, the two boy hunters called loudly half a dozen times. No answer was returned.

"Perhaps he's deaf," suggested Whopper.

"More likely he doesn't want to show himself."

"Maybe it's a she, Shep."

"Possibly. If it's a woman she must be a regular witch. Let us call again."

They did so. At first they heard nothing in return. Then came a strange sound from the cabin, and for one brief instant a dark, impish face showed itself at the broken window. Then the face disappeared and a stone came whizzing toward the lads' heads. They ducked just in time, or one or the other might have been seriously hurt.

"Let's get out—no use of staying here to be a target!" cried Whopper, who was growing nervous. "No telling what that fellow—or woman—may do next. Might come for us with a carving knife!" And he hurried away, with the doctor's son beside him. They did not slacken their pace until the dilapidated cabin had disappeared from view.

"Did you see him—or her?" asked Shep.

"Just about and no more. What a dried-up, hateful face!"

"Just what I thought. I'll wager that that person, whoever he or she is, is as mad as a—a crazy person can be."

"I believe you, and I don't know as I want to go near that cabin again."

"We ought to tell the authorities about it, though. That person might kill somebody some day."

"Well, we can tell the police when we go back."

"Could it be some tramp, who is living on farmers' chickens and the like?"

"It might be. But I think it's somebody who's crazy. A tramp wouldn't find it any fun to live away out here. Why, it must be two miles, at least, to the nearest farm."

"More like three."

"Tramps like to stay near the farms and near railroads. No, that's some kind of a crazy hermit."

Discussing the happening from every point of view, the two lads trudged on. It was now growing dark rapidly, and they were anxious to reach Firefly Lake.

"Hope we haven't missed the way," said the doctor's son presently. "Seems to me we ought to be getting to the river or the lake soon."

"Here's a rise of ground. I'm going up there and take a look," answered his chum.

From the small hill they made out the glint of water in the distance, and they also saw the glare of the camp fire Snap and Giant had started.

"Might as well steer straight for the camp fire," said Shep. "It will save us some walking."

When within a few hundred feet of the camp they set up a loud whistle, to which the others immediately responded. Then Snap and Giant came to meet them, and relieved them of some of the things. A little later all were seated around the camp fire.

"So you got through all O.K., eh?" said the doctor's son, after

Snap and Giant had told their story. "Well, so did we—but we had some queer things happen." And then he and Whopper told of the tumbles, and of what had occurred at the old cabin in the woods.

"Say, wish I had been along!" cried Snap. "I'd like to investigate that cabin and see who is there."

"You wouldn't want to investigate a block of wood or a stone thrown at your head, would you?" demanded Whopper sarcastically.

"Maybe we could go there when the hermit—or whatever he or she is—is asleep," went on Snap. He always believed in getting at the bottom of a mystery.

"If you go there you'll go without me," declared Whopper firmly. "I wouldn't tempt that—er—crazy fellow again for a billion dollars! Why, he might come out and carve a chap all up with a butcher knife, or blow your head off with a gun!"

Supper was ready, and while they were talking the young hunters managed to stow away a hearty meal, after, which all felt better. But the experiences of the day had worn them out, and each was glad enough to retire early.

"We want to be stirring early to-morrow," said the doctor's son. "We want to go up the lake and then begin to tote the outfit over the hills to the mountains."

"How about it—going to set a guard?" asked Giant.

"Wonder if we can't put Wags on guard?" asked Snap.

"I think he'd bark if anything came to disturb us," came from Whopper.

"We'll tie him to the front tent pole," said the doctor's son. "Then he won't be able to run off, and more than likely he'll bark if anything goes wrong."

They fixed the camp fire and then tied the collie fast by a cord slipped under his collar. Evidently Wags was used to this treatment, for he did not seem to mind it in the least. The young hunters entered the tent, and in less than a quarter of an hour all were sound asleep.

Thus an hour passed. Then, of a sudden, all the lads found themselves wide awake. Wags was barking furiously, and the hair of his body seemed to be fairly standing on end.

CHAPTER XI

A STRANGE MEETING

"Something is wrong!" cried Snap, leaping up and feeling for his gun. "What is it, Wags?"

The dog kept on barking and commenced to tug on the cord that held him.

"Shall I let him loose?" asked Whopper. All the boys were now on their feet, and he and Giant were rubbing their eyes. The wind had shifted and was blowing the smoke of the smoldering camp fire toward the tent.

"Don't do it—yet," answered the doctor's son. "He might bite somebody. Let us go outside first."

"Maybe it's that crazy hermit," suggested Whopper, and gave a little shiver. He could still see that impish face glaring at him. "Be careful."

One after another the young hunters stepped into the open, each with his gun ready for use. Shep stirred up the camp fire and threw on some lightwood, causing a renewed blaze.

"I don't see anything wrong," said Shep after a long look around.

"See any wild beasts?" asked Giant. "Wags would bark at a

wild beast, I am sure."

"Nothing in sight now."

All walked completely around the tent and the camp fire, but failed to see anything out of the ordinary. The collie had now ceased barking and was wagging his tail, apparently as happy and free from anxiety as ever.

"The dog must have dreamed he heard something," grumbled Whopper. "Hang the luck! I was so sleepy!" And he yawned broadly, setting his chums to doing likewise.

"Well, dogs do dream sometimes," admitted the doctor's son. "But what made him bark so loudly and look so mad?"

Nobody could answer that question, and nobody tried. They took another look around the tent, fixed the fire again, and at last one by one retired to rest once more, Wags at the foot of the tent pole as before.

It was broad daylight when they awoke again, and for a while nobody felt like stirring. At length Snap looked at his watch.

"Great mackerel!" he ejaculated. "Eight o'clock! Time we were getting breakfast and moving."

"That's so," answered Shep. "Still, there is no great hurry. Our time is our own. That's the charm of such an outing as this."

"I think we might stay here to-day," came from Giant. "It will give us a chance to rest up and to fish. Remember, we won't have much fishing after we get to the mountains."

"We can get brook trout," answered Whopper. "But just the same I'm willing to stay here to-day and fish. Maybe we can get some big maskalonge, same as we did before."

"And if we can't get those we can get some pickerel and bass and perch," added Giant.

Snap had promised to get breakfast ready, and he set in with a will as soon as he was dressed. While he was working Giant and Whopper walked down to a cove, where the boat had been left, to look over their rods and lines. The doctor's son busied himself with a camera, determined to take a few pictures before leaving the lake shore.

Suddenly there came from the cove a hurried shouting that instantly attracted the attention of Snap and Shep.

"What are they saying?" demanded the doctor's son.

"I don't know—something about the boat," answered Snap, and dropping the coffee-pot he held he ran toward the lake. Shep set the camera on a box and followed.

When they arrived at the cove they found Giant and Whopper gazing up and down and across the water in perplexity. The rowboat, with the larger portion of their outfit, was nowhere to be seen.

"Where's the boat?" demanded Snap.

"That's what we want to know," answered Giant.

"Didn't you leave it tied up?"

"Certainly I did—to this elderberry bush."

"Well, where is it now

"Don't ask me."

"Did Giant tie the boat?" asked the doctor's son. He had not seen the craft since the parting at the rapids.

"Yes, I did—and I tied it good and fast, too," answered the

small youth. "Snap saw me do it."

"Yes, I saw him tie it up, but I thought maybe he shifted the boat afterward."

"No, I left it just as it was tied up."

The boy hunters looked blankly at one another. All gazed up and down the shore and across the lake.

"Maybe Ham Spink—" began Snap.

"If he took our boat I'll—I'll kick him full of holes!" cried Giant. He had not forgotten how Spink and his cronies had annoyed them in the past.

"I don't see any footprints around here," remarked the doctor's son, looking over the ground carefully.

"Here's a tree branch broken," said Whopper.

"They might have come in a boat and towed our craft away," suggested Snap.

"Boys, I know why Wags barked during the night!" cried Giant. "He heard somebody at the boat."

"Yes, and we didn't know enough to come down here," added Snap bitterly. "If we had come we could have caught the boat-stealers redhanded."

A lively discussion followed, but it did nothing toward enlightening the boy hunters. The one fact remained that the boat and a large portion of the outfit were gone, and unless the craft could be recovered their outing would come to a premature finish.

"All I can think of to do is to take our guns and walk up and down the lake front," said the doctor's son. "Two can go one way, and two the other. If you see anything, shout or fire a gun."

"Shall we have breakfast first?" asked Snap, "It's started."

"Might as well, since we don't know how long this search will last."

Much disappointed, the chums walked back to the camp fire and there made a hasty meal of cold partridge, crackers, cheese and coffee. They left Wags tied to the tent pole.

"Maybe he'll scare off intruders—if any come," said Shep.

It was decided that Snap and Shep should go up the shore and Giant and Whopper down in the direction of the river leading to Lake Cameron. All started off briskly, anxious to catch sight of their craft as speedily as possible, or learn what had become of it.

It was comparatively easy to walk along the shore of Firefly Lake, and Snap and the doctor's son made good progress. They passed the camp, receiving a joyous bark from Wags, and then skirted a small bay leading to a fine, sandy beach.

"Fine spot for a swim," remarked Snap. "We ought to have one before we go to the mountains."

"Yes; but let us find the boat first."

"Of course."

Half an hour's walking brought the two churns to another bay. They were walking behind a fringe of bushes, and now the doctor's son stepped forward, parted the branches and peered eagerly out on the bosom of the lake.

"Hello!" he cried, with something of joy in his voice.

"Is it the boat?"

"Yes!"

And now Snap came forward.

"There it is, just rounding yonder bend of the shore. Hurry up! We'll catch the rascal who is running off with it!"

They had seen the craft, piled high with their outfit. A single person was at the oars—a boy, by his size. He was pulling leisurely.

"Maybe he won't come ashore; and we can't follow him out on the lake," said Snap.

"We won't have to follow him."

"But if he won't come in?"

"We'll make him," and the doctor's son raised his shotgun significantly.

"That's so; I forgot about our guns. Of course he'll come in if we threaten to shoot him."

The boys quickened their footsteps and soon reached a point opposite to where the rowboat was moving along.

"Hi, you, stop!" yelled Shep loudly. "Stop, I say!"

At the command the boy in the boat ceased rowing and looked around curiously.

"Who called?" he asked in a low but distinct voice.

"I did," went on the doctor's son. "Turn in here with that boat and be quick about it. What do you mean by running off with our property?"

"Why, I declare!" gasped Snap as he caught a good look at the face of the lad in the rowboat. "Shep, do you recognize him? He's the lad from the circus—the young acrobat who ran away!"

Captain Ralph Bonehill

CHAPTER XII

THE CIRCUS BOY'S STORY

Snap was right; it was indeed the youthful circus performer. He looked as thin as ever, but his face bore a far more healthy color than when the young hunters had seen him before.

"I say, what do you mean by running off with our boat?" repeated the doctor's son wrathfully.

"Is this your boat?" asked the circus boy calmly.

"It is."

"I didn't run off with it. I found it drifting along the shore, and I took off my shoes and socks and waded in after it."

"You didn't run off with it?" asked Snap.

"I give you my word of honor," replied the boy quickly. He ran the boat to shore and stepped out. "If it's your property, I'm glad to hand it over to you. I—Say, didn't I see you somewhere before?" he demanded excitedly.

I rather guess you did—at the circus, replied Shep.

"Oh! You were the fellows who—who talked to Jones, the ringmaster."

"Exactly. And you're the chap who ran away."

"That's true, I did run away. Can you blame me? They half starved me and beat me, and wanted me to go up on the trapeze after I had had a spell of sickness."

"We saw you on a freight train leaving Rallings."

"Oh, did you? Yes, I left town on a freight. It was the easiest way to go—and the cheapest." And the boy smiled quietly.

"Now give us the truth about our boat," said Shep sternly. "You ran off with it last night, didn't you?"

"No, sir!" And the boy looked the doctor's son squarely in the eyes. "I never took any property that didn't belong to me in my life."

"And where did you find the boat?"

"About half a mile from here, along the shore. I made up my mind it had broken loose somehow, and I thought if I found the owner he might—er—that is—"

"Give you a reward?" suggested Snap. Something about the lad's manner pleased him.

"Well, he might give me something to eat."

"Hungry?"

The boy nodded.

"Well, we'll give you something to eat—all you want—if you are quite sure you didn't take the boat," answered the doctor's son.

"I told you the truth."

"Then get into the boat again, and we'll row to our camp."

The three got in, the strange boy sitting in the stern. Shep and Snap took up the oars and soon the craft was heading for the cove where it had been tied up the night before. A shot was fired to notify Giant and Whopper that the boat had been found.

"What's your name?" asked Snap on the way.

"Tommy Cabot; but up to the show they called me Buzz."

"Are your folks with the circus?"

"My folks are dead—that is, my father and mother are. I've got a sister somewhere, older than myself, but I don't know just where she is."

"How did you happen to go with the circus?" asked Shep.

"They picked me up at Centerport. They saw that I was limber and could do a turn or two, and they made me join. They promised me good wages and a fine time, but as soon as we got on the road they treated me worse than my dog."

"Your dog?"

"Yes. I had a dog, and I said I wouldn't join unless they took the dog, too. Jones wanted me to give him, the dog—he was a fine collie—but I wouldn't do it, and when I left I took my dog with me."

"Where is he now?"

"I don't know. He ran away several days ago, and I haven't seen him since."

"And he was a collie?" asked Snap.

"Yes." Tommy Cabot's eyes brightened expectantly. "You haven't seen him, have you? He must be somewhere around these lakes."

"We found a dog—a collie. He's got a tag on his collar—number 444."

"My dog!" cried the circus boy. "Oh, I'll be glad to see him! He's my best friend, even if he did run away. Anyway, I guess he went to get something to eat. I hadn't much for him."

"What do you call your dog?" asked the doctor's son.

"Wags—because he moves his tail so much."

"Well, I never! That's what we dubbed him."

"Tell me," broke in Snap. "Do you know what happened at the circus after you left?"

"I heard that some of the animals got away. I didn't hear the particulars. I went down among the farms and laid low, waiting for the circus to go east."

"A lion got away, and also Abe, the educated chimpanzee. The circus folks think those men who were discharged and you were responsible."

"Me! I didn't do it, and I never had anything to do with those men who were discharged. They were a hard crowd."

A little later the camp was gained. As soon as the dog saw Tommy Cabot he became frantic with joy and leaped up and licked the hand of his youthful master. Tommy fairly hugged Wags to his breast.

Of course, Whopper and Giant were surprised to see the circus boy and glad to know the boat had been found. How the craft had gotten loose was a mystery nobody was able to solve.

A substantial breakfast was prepared for the circus boy, and while he was eating he told his story in detail—how his parents had died years before, and how his sister Grace had been taken by some friends in the Middle West.

"I sold papers and blacked boots for a living, and I learned to do handsprings and the like," said Tommy. "Then the circus came along and I went with it, taking Wags. Some of the circus men were kind to me, but most of them were rough, and Jones and Casso were cruel. When I ran away I made up my mind I'd never go back, but would try to get work in some city and also try to find my sister Grace. But I ran short of money and then I came out here, thinking I could get work on some farm, or go with some sportsmen to carry their traps for 'em. But I didn't find any farms out here, and the only sportsmen I met were some well-dressed young fellows who jeered me and called me a scarecrow—I suppose on account of my shabby clothes." The circus boy still wore the big suit of rags the young hunters had noticed before.

"Must have been Ham Spink and his crowd," murmured Whopper. "It would be just like them to do that."

In spite of the color in his cheeks the young hunters could see that the circus lad was far from strong. He was nervous, and evidently needed plenty of food and a rest.

Having heard the runaway's tale, Snap and the others told something about themselves. Tommy listened with keen interest, and presently his eyes showed considerable enthusiasm.

"I wish I was going with you," he said. "Such an outing would suit me down to the ground. I can cook some, and I could wash the dishes and cut wood and keep the camp in order, and all that. But I don't suppose you'd want me along in these old duds." And he looked sadly at his torn and faded suit, so much too big for him.

"Oh, we might fit you out with a sweater and a cap," said Snap. The more he saw of the circus boy the better he liked the young fellow. "But I don't know," he added hastily, looking at his chums.

"We didn't expect to take anybody," said the doctor's son slowly. "But you might stay with us for a day or two, anyway—and we can talk it over. We ought to be better acquainted before we make a bargain."

"He could help us take our outfit to the mountains," said Giant. "We could pay him for the work."

"I don't want any pay. Just give me my meals, and it will be all right."

"We can settle the whole thing later," said Shep. "But you can stay for the present."

"Wasn't it queer?" cried Whopper. "We found your dog and you found our boat!"

"It was queer—but I'm glad of it, for it kind of squares up," answered the circus boy. "I don't know how much you think of your boat, but I think a whole lot of Wags."

"If we hadn't got the boat back our outing would have been spoiled," said the doctor's son. "But come; if we are going fishing, let us start at once. We can do the rest of our talking after our lines are in."

CHAPTER XIII

SOME FINE FISHING

The four boy hunters were soon down at the lake shore preparing their hooks and lines. Tommy Cabot went along, and while they fished he sat and watched them.

"This beats being with a circus all hollow," said the young acrobat.

"I always thought circus life was fine," declared Giant.

"It is—on the outside. But on the inside! No more of it for me!"

"Did they pay you much?" questioned Whopper.

"I was supposed to get ten dollars a week, but I didn't. Every time payday came around they'd deduct something for extras I had had and things they said I had broken, or torn, or lost, so I usually got two or three dollars, and that I had to spend on clothing, shoes—and eating, for the meals weren't heavy at the show. Then, one night, some scamp stole my suit, and I had to buy these from one of the workmen. I got 'em cheap, but they aren't much good," and Tommy smiled grimly as he surveyed the dilapidated garments.

At fishing the boys were highly successful. Snap caught the first fish—a good-sized perch—and the doctor's son followed with a fine pickerel. Then came Whopper with another pickerel. For a while Giant caught nothing.

"What's the matter, Giant?" queried Snap. "You are usually our best angler."

"Oh, wait; I haven't begun yet," returned the small youth.

Scarcely had he spoken when he felt a tug and commenced to play a fish with vigor. That it was a large specimen of the finny tribe was evident by the way the rod bent and the line snapped and hummed.

"Look out, or you'll lose him!" cried Whopper excitedly.

"Let Giant alone—he knows how to play any fish," said Snap.

"That's what!" added the doctor's son.

The others forgot their lines in watching Giant. Up came the line for fifty feet, and then out it would rush. But at last he commenced to reel in steadily, and then, with a swing, he lifted his catch bodily and allowed it to drop on the grass, where it flounced and flopped vigorously for a moment.

"A maskalonge!" cried the other boys simultaneously.

"And a big one!" added Whopper.

"Tell you what! It takes Giant to haul in the big fish!" was Snap's comment. "No little chaps for him!"

The catching of the maskalonge enthused all, and they went to fishing with renewed vigor. By dinner-time they had eighteen fish to their credit, a few little ones and some weighing two and three pounds.

"Say, you fellows will have plenty of fish to eat," remarked the boy from the circus.

Captain Ralph Bonehill

"Well, you shall have your share," added Snap quickly. "Which puts me in mind that it must be near feeding time."

"Shall I get some wood and start up the fire?" asked Tommy.

"If you will."

At once the circus boy started off, and when the others got back to camp they found a fine blaze going with plenty of wood near by to keep it up. Tommy was washing the left-over dishes, and had set a kettle of water to boil.

"He certainly isn't lazy," whispered Snap to Shep. "If we take him along he'll earn his food."

"Yes, and if he does the camp work that will give us more time to rest and take pictures," returned the doctor's son.

"Boys, I move we take a swim this afternoon," cried Giant, while they were sitting around waiting for some fish to cook. "It will be our last chance before going to the mountains, and the water is just right."

"Second the motion!" returned Snap.

"So say we all of us!" sang out Whopper. "I've been dying for a swim for the last ten years!"

"Dying again! Poor boy!" sighed Shep. "Now, if you'll only live—"

He got no further, for, coming up behind him, Whopper pulled him over on the grass. As he went rolling he caught his tormentor by the ankles and down came Whopper. Then over and over rolled both lads, up against Giant, who joined in the tussle good-naturedly.

"Look out for the fire!" yelled Snap, and as they rolled close to the flames he tried to force them back. Then down he went himself, and the mix-up became more strenuous than ever. It was good, healthy fun, and Tommy Cabot stood by with a broad grin on his face, enjoying it thoroughly. As they rolled toward the woods he picked up an armful of leaves and scattered it over the crowd. The tussle lasted for full five minutes, and then the various boys sat up almost exhausted.

"Guess you've got an appetite for dinner now," observed the boy from the circus.

"Appetite!" cried Whopper. "I could eat a house and lot!"

"With the fence and barn thrown in," added Giant.

They washed up a bit and soon had dinner, consisting of baked maskalonge, pancakes and chocolate. For dessert they had apples.

"Now we'll rest for an hour and then go swimming," said Shep, and so it was decided. All took a nap, Tommy lying down on the grass with the faithful Wags beside him.

While fishing the boys had selected a spot for swimming, where the bottom was sloping and sandy. They went in together, the circus boy with the others.

"You can swim?" asked Snap.

"Oh, yes. And if I couldn't Wags would take care of me," answered Tommy. "Just see him tow me!" And getting a stick he called the collie. Wags took hold of the end and commenced to swim along, dragging his young master after him.

"Hurrah for Wags!" shouted Whopper. "When I get tired I'll have him haul me along for a while." Evidently the collie enjoyed the bath as much as did the boys.

They remained in the water for the best part of an hour,

racing, diving and doing various "stunts." When they came out Snap declared it was the best swim he had ever had.

"It's a pity we won't be able to swim in the mountains," said Giant.

"Well, we can't expect to have everything," returned the doctor's son.

Having dried off and dressed, the boys returned to camp and spent the rest of the afternoon in getting ready to move early in the morning. It was decided to hide the boat in the bushes and leave a portion of their outfit in the craft, tied down under the tarpaulin. They would carry with them all the things needed for several days, so that a second trip would not be necessary until they felt like taking it.

"I'll carry a share," said Tommy. "I'm feeling stronger than I was."

"We'll give you a small load," answered the doctor's son.

They retired early and were up at sunrise. Tommy renewed the camp fire, and they had a meal of fish and wheatcakes, with coffee. Then the tent was taken down and packed along with the other things.

"Now put out the fire and we'll be off," said Shep, and he saw to it personally that every spark of the blaze was extinguished. As my old readers know, the boy hunters knew only too well what a forest fire meant, and they had no desire to start such a conflagration.

Their route now lay over some hills that were more or less strange to them. But they had received many instructions from Jed Sanborn, and thought they would have little trouble in gaining a trail back of the hills that led into the Windy Mountains.

"Are the mountains really windy?" asked Snap as they began the climb up the hills back of the lake, each with a good-sized load strapped to his back.

"They are only windy at certain times of the year," answered the doctor's son. "But when it blows, why, it blows, so Jed Sanborn said."

"Then we'll have to put our tent up good and strong," came from Whopper. "We don't want to wake up some night and find ourselves blown into the middle of next year!"

"And dying to know how we are going to get back," added Giant dryly.

"Giant, if you say dying again—" began Whopper.

"Save your wind, boys!" interrupted Shep. "We've got a long and hard climb before us."

What the doctor's son said about the climb was true—the way was a steady pull upward, and they had frequently to stop to get their breath. It was nearly eleven o'clock when they reached the top of the hill. They had been on the upgrade for three hours.

"Let us rest until after dinner," said Snap. "No use killing ourselves."

"We've still got some miles to go," answered Shep.

"I know it—but it will be mostly down grade—at least, until we reach the foot of the mountains."

It was decided to rest, and all of the young hunters willingly slipped their loads and sat down. Below them was Firefly Lake, with Lake Cameron in the distance on one side and Lake Narsac in the distance on the other. Back of them lay the Windy Mountains, with a hollow of trees and bushes between.

The boys viewed the mountains with interest, thinking of the outing they hoped to have there.

CHAPTER XIV

AFTER DEER WITH GUN AND CAMERA

"I hope we strike a good camping spot by night," said Snap, "for, unless I miss my guess, it will rain before morning."

"Oh, don't say rain!" cried Giant. "We can do without rain."

"It may not be a lasting storm, but some rain will come, mark my words."

"I think I see the trail up the mountains," said Whopper, who was looking through a pair of fieldglasses. "Anyway, it's path of some kind."

The others gave a look, and all decided that Whopper was right.

Resuming their loads after the noonday repast, they started down the hill in the direction of Windy Mountains. They had some big bare rocks to cover, and slipped and slid over these as best they could, and then plunged straight into a thick woods.

"Ought to be hunting here, if anywhere," observed Shep. "Looks as if it was new ground for sportsmen."

"Beware of sink holes!" cried Whopper as he reached a rather soft spot. "We don't want to go down as we did the other time we were out."

"Look!" exclaimed the doctor's son as they came to a small opening in the woods. "Deer, or I'll eat my cap!"

He pointed to some bushes and tender saplings growing near. The bushes had been nibbled, and so had the bark on the saplings, showing that some animal had been there.

"I believe you are right, and if so we may get a shot," answered Giant.

"Yes, a shot—but not until after we have used our cameras," answered the doctor's son. "Don't forget the first object of this outing—to get some good pictures."

"Right you are, Shep; I forgot. But we must shoot the deer— after we have our photos."

"Better sight the game first," came from Snap.

With the thoughts of bringing down one or more deer filling their minds, the boy hunters did not care so much about making a camp for the night. If necessary, they knew they could erect their tent anywhere, and take it down again in the morning. Even the prospect of rain did not daunt them.

"Let us hurry," said Shep. "If we reach the deer we want to do it while it is light enough to take some pictures."

With their cameras and guns ready for use, they went on, Tommy cautioning the dog to be silent. Wags seemed to understand and even acted as if he might lead them to the game. But he was not trained, so they took no chances on this.

Deep in a hollow they came upon the unmistakable hoofmarks of three deer. They followed these through the woods and to a small clearing. At a clump of bushes the doctor's son called a halt.

"I think they may be near," he whispered. "If so, we want to go slow or they'll get away from us."

"Perhaps you'd better go ahead and take a look," said Snap, sure that that was what his chum desired.

The loads were slipped to the ground, and they went on, Shep well in advance. Suddenly the doctor's son put up one hand. It was a signal that the game was in sight. Snap whispered to Tommy to stop and hold the collie.

"There they are, by yonder rocks," said the doctor's son, pointing with his finger. "We can all get good pictures, I think. Let us spread out a little."

They did as he advised. The three deer were close together, grazing. The boys came up almost breathlessly, and each snapped his camera for two films or plates. At the first clicking one of the deer, evidently the leader, raised his head. Scenting the air, he made a beautiful sight. For just an instant he stood still, then gave a snort and started to run.

"Shoot 'em!" cried Shep, and swinging his camera out of the way he caught up his firearm. But Snap was ahead of him, and bang! went his piece. Bang! bang! bang! went the others in rapid succession. Then Wags began to bark furiously, and Tommy let him go. After the game he leaped at his topmost speed.

The first volley from the shotguns laid one of the deer low, while a second was slightly wounded, and began to limp away. The other deer kept on running and soon disappeared into the dense forest.

"Come on—let us get that wounded deer!" cried Whopper.

"There goes Wags after him!" shouted Tommy.

"That dog will get killed if he doesn't look out," answered Snap, who knew only too well how a cornered deer can fight.

But Wags was too wise to get within reach of the deer's hoofs and head. He raced around and around the game, simply worrying it.

Coming closer, the boy hunters watched their chances and Snap took another shot, followed by Giant. These were fatal, and limping a few feet farther, the deer staggered and fell, and soon breathed its last.

"Call off the dog," ordered the doctor's son. But this was unnecessary, for after a single sniff Wags retired and did not attempt to molest the game.

"Talk about luck!" cried Whopper, swinging his cap in the air. "I call this prime! Two deer, first crack out of the box!"

"Yes; and see the fine pictures we got," added Snap. "That is, I trust they are all right," he added hastily.

"Did you change your films and plates?" asked the doctor's son.

All had, and they guarded jealously those containing the precious exposures.

"Now we must take some more photos," said Shep. "We'll get Tommy to snap us holding up the deer on poles. We can label the two pictures 'Before Shooting' and 'After.'"

"That's the stuff!" cried Giant slangily.

Two poles were soon cut and a deer slung on each, and while Shep and Snap raised up one, Whopper and Giant raised the other. Tommy had been instructed as to what to do, and he took a snapshot or a time picture with each camera, so that they would have plenty of films and plates, in case one or more proved failures.

"It's a bit extravagant," said the doctor's son. "But we'll not have such game pictures every day. When we simply take scenery one plate or one film will do."

"When we make camp we can hang the deer in front of the tent and get another view," said Snap.

"Yes; and get a view of our big string of fish, before we eat 'em all up," added Giant.

"Well, one thing is certain," said Whopper, after they had surveyed their prizes thoroughly; "we can't get to the Windy Mountains by to-night with such a load."

"In that case we might as well make two bites of the trip and camp here for to-night," said Shep. "I reckon this spot is as good as any. There's a brook with good water, for the deer have been using it."

"There's another reason for going into camp," came from Snap. "Just look at the sky over to the west."

All gazed in the direction mentioned and saw heavy black clouds just showing over the treetops. The clouds advanced rapidly, soon covering the sun. Then came the rumble of distant thunder.

"A thunderstorm!" exclaimed Tommy. "I don't like them at all. What shall we do?"

"Put up the tent as quickly as we can," ordered the doctor's son. "That storm may last all night, and we want to keep dry if we can."

In great haste they selected some saplings and cut them down for tent poles and pegs. Then they got out the canvas and put it up, driving in the pegs that held it as deeply as possible. The tent was erected on some sloping ground, and behind it they cut a V in the soil, so that the water might run off on either side instead of across the flooring of the shelter. Then they cut some brushwood for couches and hauled it inside.

"Here comes the storm!" cried Snap presently, and scarcely had he spoken when there came a rush of wind, followed by some big drops of rain. Then came more wind, swaying the tent violently and causing the sides to bulge out like a balloon. A torrent of water followed, and all of the boys were glad enough to crawl under the tent and tie the opening in front tight shut behind them.

CHAPTER XV

IN THE MOUNTAINS AT LAST

The boys and even the dog put in a thoroughly uncomfortable night. It thundered and lightened for two hours, and for the larger portion of the time the downpour was so heavy that it was impossible for the V-shaped trench behind the tent to carry it off. Consequently, some of the water rushed directly across the flooring of the shelter, wetting the brushwood cut for sleeping purposes. To keep their shoes and socks dry, the young hunters went barefooted. Once the wind cut loose a corner of the tent, and, despite the rain, Shep and Snap had to go out and cut longer pegs with which to fasten the ropes. They had on rubber coats, but still got a good deal of water in their faces and down their necks.

It was impossible to light a camp fire, and so they had to eat a cold supper of such things as chanced to be handy. They could not lie down, and had to sit on little stacks of the damp brushwood, with their bare feet in the water and mud.

"Say, this is dead loads of fun!" was Whopper's sarcastic comment. "Just as funny as doing an example in algebra or writing a composition on the decay of the Roman Empire!"

"Are you dying to—" began Giant, when a vigorous pinch on the arm from Whopper stopped him. "Wow! Let up!"

"Then you let up."

"I will."

By midnight the worst of the storm was over, but it still rained steadily, and this kept up until almost daybreak. But then the wind shifted and the clouds scattered rapidly. Utterly worn out, the boys leaned against the tent poles and caught such "cat naps" as they could.

When the young hunters finally emerged from the tent a surprise awaited them. Tommy was ahead of them, and the circus boy had cut such dry wood as he could find and started a big blaze. More than this, he had put on a kettle of water to boil.

"Good for you, Tommy!" cried the doctor's son. "We'll soon have a hot cup of coffee to cheer us, and we can dry out the tent and our clothing while we get breakfast."

"That's about the worst night I can remember," said Whopper. "My! how it did pour at first! I thought sure we'd be washed down into some hillside torrent and into the lake."

They placed all the damp things close to the fire to dry, and put on their socks and shoes. Then Giant and Whopper, assisted by Tommy, prepared a rather elaborate breakfast of fish and venison steaks.

"We deserve a square meal," said Giant. "It will put new vigor into us." And his words proved true. By the time they had finished the repast they were ready to joke over the discomforts through which they had passed.

"But one storm is enough," said Snap. "I trust it stays clear after this."

The woods were so wet it was decided not to travel through them until after dinner. The sun came out strongly, and in the clear sky thus presented the boys managed to get several pleasing photographs. One was of Tommy and his dog sitting on a rock, and this was so good that, when shown later, it was very much admired. They also took a photograph of Giant and Whopper with the strings of fish.

Late that afternoon found them at the foot of the Windy Mountains. Here they discovered a well-defined trail and also a signboard, telling them the game preserve in which Dr. Reed was interested was just beyond."

"Now we haven't much farther to go," said the doctor's son. "My father said we'd find a good camping spot less than a mile from here."

"I'm glad of it," answered Giant. "This load on my back isn't as light as it might be."

Pushing on, they soon came to where another signboard had been located; but the board had been knocked off with a stone or a hammer and was missing.

"Some hunter's meanness," was Snap's comment.

"A fellow who would destroy a signboard ought to be locked up," was Whopper's comment. "It's about on a par with starting a forest fire."

They trudged on, and presently came to where somebody had had a camp fire. Here were some empty tins and some well-picked bones. Giant kicked over one of the empty tins.

"Hello! I know who was here!" he cried. "Ham Spink and his crowd."

"How do you know?" demanded the doctor's son.

"Because I know they had some of this brand of canned goods with 'em—saw it among their supplies. It's different from the kind we have, or what you can get in the regular stores. The Spinks have their goods sent by freight from the city."

"Giant must be right," said Snap. "And look here, will you?"

As he spoke Snap pulled from the dead embers of the fire a half-burned bit of wood. It was part of a signboard.

"Humph! the signboard that was missing below here," muttered Shep. "Ham and his crowd were too lazy to cut firewood, so they used the board. If that isn't the height of laziness and meanness!"

"It's against the law to destroy signboards," said Whopper. "That crowd ought to be brought to book for this."

"If you said anything they'd say we did it," responded Snap. "Ham would do anything to keep out of trouble and get us into a muss."

"That camp fire was built after the storm," said the doctor's son. "That proves the Spink crowd can't be far from here."

"If they are near us we want to be on our guard," observed Giant. "They'd like no better fun than to steal our things. They haven't forgotten what happened on the lakes this summer and last winter."

The boy hunters were bound for a spot mentioned to them by Dr. Reed and Jed Sanborn. It was a small "dent" in the mountain side, where were located a fine spring of cool water with a rocky brook beyond. Some distance farther was a cut in the mountain with a tiny lake, surrounded by cedars and called Cedar Lake.

It was nightfall when they reached the "dent" and the spring. All were thirsty, and the sparkling water was very refreshing.

"Father says that some day he'll organize a company to bottle this water," said Shep. "He is sure it will command a large sale in the big cities—it is so clear and pure."

"It couldn't be better," answered Snap. He looked around him. "And what an ideal spot for our camp!"

It assuredly was ideal in every respect. They could see for miles to the east, south and west, over hill after hill, covered with green trees and brushwood, with ribbons of water between, and here and there a lake. Using the field-glasses they could make out the church steeple of Fairview and some other buildings. Between the hills they could see various farms, with the cattle grazing in the pastures, or standing in groups in the barnyards. All was as silent and as calm as one could wish.

"What a place for a castle, like those of old!" murmured Snap as his eyes roamed over the scene. "Just think of this in the light of the full moon."

"Snap is getting romantic," came from Whopper. "Come on down to the earth, sonny, and help pitch the tent, or you'll have to sleep out in that moonlight to-night and run the risk of getting moonstruck." And this remark brought forth a laugh, in which even Snap joined.

As tired as they were, the five boys cut the necessary poles and hoisted the tent. As this was to be a permanent camp for some weeks they erected the shelter with care, and around it dug a deep trench, with another trench to carry rain down the mountain side, so that none might run over the flooring as it had during the thunderstorm. Then they spent considerable time in cutting down some heavy cedar boughs for bedding. Snap, Whopper and Tommy did this latter work, and while it was going on Shep and Giant got together some flat stones and built something of a fireplace and a stove, not far from the tent's entrance. Then they cut firewood and soon had a generous blaze started and put the kettle on to boil.

"And are we going to stay here for a while, and just hunt and fish and—and rest?" asked the boy from the circus.

"Yes," answered Shep. "Don't you like it?"

"Like it! I think it's the—the best ever! Couldn't be better!" was the hearty reply.

"I think it will make you fat and strong, Tommy, and that's what you need."

"And another thing," answered the boy. "Those circus people can't find me out here."

"It's not likely."

Everybody was glad that a permanent camp had been reached at last, and that night all slept "like rocks," to use Giant's way of expressing it. They left Wags on guard, but this was unnecessary, for nothing came to disturb them.

The next day was spent in perfecting the camp and in taking care of what remained of the fish and of the venison. The skins were nailed up in the sun to dry. The boys were sorry they could not keep all of the meat, but this was impossible, as they had no ice and no means of smoking or pickling it.

"Here comes somebody!" cried Whopper, while they sat around waiting for supper, which Snap and Tommy were preparing. Two boys were approaching, and as they came closer the young hunters recognized Ham Spink and his close crony, Carl Dudder.

CHAPTER XVI

A VISIT FROM THE ENEMY

"Wonder what they want?" whispered Shep as the newcomers drew closer.

"Perhaps they have only come out of idle curiosity," returned Snap.

"Well, in that case, they had better stay away," grumbled Giant.

Ham Spink and Carl Dudder came up slowly. To tell the truth, they were a bit afraid, thinking the others might jump on them and begin a fight, because of what had happened at the Fairview dock.

"Hello!" said Ham presently. He did not know how else to start a conversation.

"Hello yourself!" responded the doctor's son shortly.

"Going to camp out here, eh?" went on the dudish youth.

"Oh, no; we've opened an oyster house," returned Whopper, who was bound to have his fun.

"Humph! Frank Dawson, you needn't get funny!"

"Was I funny? I didn't see you laugh."

"You know what I mean."

"Expect to do some big hunting, I suppose?" said Carl Dudder with a bit of a sneer in his tones.

"We generally do pretty well when we are out," responded Snap.

"Following us up, eh?"

"Not at all."

"Yes, you are. You knew we were coming here."

"And you know who this tract of land belongs to, now?" said the doctor's son.

"It isn't fenced in," answered Carl, and his face took on a leer. "Anybody can hunt here who wants to."

"That is true—but it will be fenced in next season. And, by the way, what right had you to tear down one of the signboards and use it for firewood?"

"Who said we did that?" demanded Ham.

"We saw the half-burned board at your camp fire."

"You can't blame that on us!" cried Carl.

"We can, and do," responded Snap. "You ought to be locked up for it."

"Oh, give us a rest!" growled Ham.

"What brought you here?" demanded Snap sharply.

"Oh, we knew we were being followed—saw you from a distance—and made up our mind to see who it was. I don't see why you can't leave us alone."

"We are not following you," said Giant, "And if you'll leave us alone we'll not bother you."

"But you have got to keep your distance," added Whopper. "No more underhanded work, like we had before. Understand?"

Ham paid no attention to the last words. He and his crony were looking at Tommy. Now they whispered together.

"Say, aren't you the kid that ran away from the circus?" demanded Ham, turning to the small youth.

At the question Tommy looked surprised and then scared.

"Wha—what do you know about me?" he stammered.

"Answer me," ordered Ham. "You ran away from Casso's Railroad Shows, didn't you?"

"Don't tell him a thing, Tommy!" cried Snap quickly. "It is none of his business."

"Ha! I knew I was right!" cried Ham triumphantly. "You're the boy they called Buzz, the Human Fly. I saw you perform at Chester, and I heard later about your running away. And you helped to let a lion and a chimpanzee escape, too."

"I did not!" cried Tommy. "The men who were discharged let those animals get away. I had nothing whatever to do with it."

"Oh, yes, that's your story; but the circus people tell it differently," put in Carl Dudder. "I was talking to one of them only the other day. They'd give a good deal to catch you and those men."

As he spoke he advanced toward Tommy as if to catch hold of the lad. The boy from the circus shrank back and looked very much alarmed.

"Here, Carl Dudder, you leave that boy alone!" cried the doctor's son. "Don't you dare to touch him!"

"I'll do as I please. The boy doesn't belong to you," blustered Carl.

"I know that—but you are not going to lay the weight of your finger on him."

"Don't do it," whispered Ham to his crony in alarm. "Remember, they are five to two."

"I think there is a reward for this boy," answered Carl in an equally low tone of voice.

"Well, if there is, keep mum and we may be able to get it."

There was an awkward pause. Tommy looked appealingly at the doctor's son and his other friends.

"Don't you worry; they shan't touch you," said Shep kindly. "They are big bullies, that's all. We know them thoroughly."

"Are you going to stay here?" asked Ham.

"That is our business," answered Snap. "Where have you located?"

"That is our business."

"So it is; but I want you to understand, once for all, Ham Spink, that this time you must keep your distance. If you try to molest us in any way you'll get the worst of it."

"How long are you going to stay?"

"That is our business, too."

"Come on, Ham," said Carl in a low voice. "What is the use of talking to them at all? Let us get back to our own camp, and let them take care of themselves."

"All right, if you say so," answered Ham Spink, and turning on his heel he walked back the way he had come, with his crony beside him.

"Now, what brought those chaps here?" demanded Snap as soon as their enemies were out of hearing. "No good, I'll wager that."

"Oh, I guess they just wanted to come and say something," said Giant. "Let us have supper. I'm too hungry to wait any longer."

Supper was had, and the boy hunters and Tommy sat around the camp fire for two hours, discussing the situation and planning what they would do for the days to come. It was decided to pay a visit to the lake for the remainder of the supplies two days later—after they had hunted and taken pictures and rested up a little.

The two days passed quickly. The boy hunters saw and heard nothing of the Spink crowd and almost forgot about them. They went out for game, and managed to bring down some rabbits, squirrels and some fine quail, and also a pinemarten. They took over a dozen pictures of the game and also of the scenery, and Shep managed to get a fine photograph of an old owl as he sat on a tree limb. The boys made no effort to shoot the owl, for he really seemed friendly and did not offer to fly away.

It was decided that Tommy and Whopper should remain at the camp while the other three made the trip to Firefly Lake.

"Take good care of things while we are gone," cautioned the

doctor's son. "Don't let the Spink crowd get the best of you."

"We'll watch out," answered Whopper. "If they try any funny business we'll shoot them into the middle of next year!"

"Oh, don't shoot anybody!" cried Snap.

"Well, you know what I mean," answered the youth who loved to exaggerate.

Shep and the others had expected to start off directly after breakfast, but Snap had to fix one of his shoes, and this delayed them. But by ten o'clock they were on the way, the others waving them a fond farewell.

"We'll look for you by to-morrow night," said Tommy.

It was an easy matter to climb down the mountain side, but the walk up the hill that separated them from the lake was another story. Yet, as they had only their guns to carry, they made good progress, and by the middle of the afternoon they were in plain sight of the body of water where they had left the boat.

"Somebody ahead of us!" cried Snap presently, and pointed out three persons walking toward the lake.

"I wonder if they can be members of the Spink crowd?" was Shep's comment. "Let us get closer and see"

CHAPTER XVII

WHAT HAPPENED UNDER THE CLIFF

It was presently made evident to our friends that the persons ahead were Ham Spink, Carl Dudder and a lad named Dick Bush, who had in former years been a close personal friend to Ham.

"Wonder where they are going?" asked Snap.

"Down to the lake," answered the doctor's son. "Most likely to where they left their boat."

"Let us keep behind them and out of sight," suggested Giant. "If they see us they may follow us up and damage our boat after we are gone."

So, although they kept the Spink crowd well in sight, they took good care not to show themselves.

Reaching the lake shore, Ham Spink and his friends came to a halt behind a clump of willows overhanging the water. Close by the others saw a rowboat tied up.

"That must be their boat," whispered Snap. "Most likely they came for the same purpose that we did—to get supplies."

"Listen!" whispered the doctor's son. "I just heard somebody mention my name."

"Their boat must be somewhere along here," they heard Ham Spink exclaim. "And if it is—We'll fix it, all right," finished Carl Dudder. "Well, that's all right," expostulated Dick Bush.

"But we don't want to do anything unlawful. They might have us arrested."

"They won't know who did it," answered Ham.

"What do you think of doing if you locate their boat?" asked Dick.

"We'll take out the supplies and hide 'em, and then fill the boat with rocks and sink her," answered Ham.

"That will be doing 'em up brown!" chuckled Carl.

"Well, I don't know about this," answered Dick Bush doubtfully. He was not quite so lawless in his ideas as were the others.

"Oh, it will be all right; we won't hurt the boat any," answered Ham. "Come on; the quicker we locate the boat the better. As soon as we've fixed their boat we can come back here and get our things and hurry back to camp." And then the three boys moved along down the lake shore.

"Well, wouldn't that jar you?" cried Snap, when the other crowd was gone. "Hide our supplies and sink our boat! Well, I guess not!"

"They haven't turned in the right direction to find our boat," returned the doctor's son. "We can get it out of the way before they come back."

"We ought to pay them for this," murmured Giant. "Let us take their boat and row it up the lake. It will give 'em something to do to find it."

"That's the talk!" cried Snap. "As the old saying goes, 'what is sauce for the goose is sauce for the gander.' Jump in and we'll take the boat to where we left our own."

They soon had the Spink rowboat untied, and leaping aboard they shoved the craft out into the lake. Then Snap and Shep took the oars, and they were soon moving up Firefly Lake. They kept close to the overhanging trees and bushes, so that the other crowd might not discover what was taking place.

The distance to where they had left their own craft was not quite half a mile, and they reached the spot in less than a quarter of an hour. They pulled inshore, to find their boat just as it had been left.

"Now, the quicker we work the better," said the doctor's son. "I've got an idea," he went on, as he caught sight of a tiny island about a hundred feet from shore. "Why not tie their boat fast over there? Then if they want it they can swim for it."

"Good!" cried Snap, and grinned.

Taking their own boat along, they rowed to the island, and there the Spink craft was made fast on the side next to the main shore and in plain view of anybody who might be passing. On the shore of the island Snap stuck up one of the oars and on the top placed a rubber boot he found in the rowboat—one of a pair Ham had brought along in case of prolonged wet weather.

"Ham will recognize that rubber boot," said Snap. "And then he'll know the boat is his." The sight of the rubber boot on the top of the oar was a comical one and the boys had to laugh as they looked at it.

Having fastened the boat so that it could not possibly drift away, the boys boarded their own craft and rowed still farther up Firefly Lake, until they came to a cove and a creek, the latter thickly overhung with bushes. They pulled the craft out of sight, so that to find it without knowing where it was located would be practically impossible.

"Now, then, to take our things and go into camp for the night," said the doctor's son. "We'll have to find some shelter under the rocks, not having a tent."

The boys knew the locality fairly well, from their previous visits, and walked to where there was a split in the hills. Here was located a rocky cliff, hollowed out somewhat at the bottom.

"We can camp here," said Shep. "With a camp fire in front the hollow will be quite comfortable."

While in the cove they had managed to catch a few perch and a pickerel, and starting a blaze, they cooked these. They had some crackers and cheese along, so made a comfortable if not an elaborate meal, washing it down with a drink from a spring.

"We ought to get to bed early," said Snap. "Then we can start back for camp at sunrise, and so get ahead of the Spink crowd."

"Oh, they won't go back until they find their boat," said Giant.

"I don't know about that," said the doctor's son. "They may get mad and lay it to us and start back to-night. You can never tell what Ham Spink and Carl Dudder will do. Dick Bush isn't quite so bad."

As it was warm, they allowed the fire to die down, and by nine o'clock all were sleeping soundly. They did not think it necessary to stand guard, for the hollow was well screened from outside observation, and they had all their traps behind them, next to the cliff.

How long he had been asleep the doctor's son did not know,

but he awoke with a start, feeling something pressing on his breast. He gave a yell of fright and alarm and added another yell as he felt his leg pulled. Then a dark body fled from the hollow and went crashing through the bushes beyond.

"Wha—what's the matter?" came in a stammering voice from Giant.

"Who was that?" demanded Snap as, in the darkness, he felt for his gun. The fire was practically out, and the hollow was intensely gloomy.

"I don't know; Ham Spink, maybe," answered the doctor's son, much bewildered. "He stood on me and pulled my foot," he added.

The boy hunters leaped up, and after some trouble armed themselves. It was dark around the cliff, so they could see nothing. They listened intently and at a distance heard a peculiar noise and the rustling of some brushwood.

"Shall I give 'em a shot?" suggested Snap.

"No; you might kill somebody," answered Shep. He raised his voice: "Hi, Ham Spink! Come back here! We know you!"

To this call no answer was vouchsafed. Again the boys listened, but now the only sound that broke the stillness was the low wind in the tree branches overhead.

"He has gone, whoever he was," said Snap. "Shep, are you sure it was Ham?"

"Not at all. I only thought it might be. For all I know it might have been a wild animal."

"What! to pull your leg?" queried Giant.

"Well, maybe he didn't really pull the leg. You see, I was pretty sound asleep. But he, or it, jumped over me and back again."

"Let's make a light and see if the outfit is O.K.," suggested Snap. They had a small pocket lantern along, and this was lit and an examination was made.

"See, the sugar bag is bursted open!" cried the doctor's son.

"The beans are scattered everywhere!" came from Giant.

"And the cracker box is open and some of the crackers are missing," added Snap. "That must have been the work of some enemy. He wanted to destroy our stores."

"But I—I really don't think it was Ham," said Shep slowly. "It was—well, it didn't seem like anybody of that crowd. I didn't get much of a look, but it wasn't like Ham, or Carl, or Dick."

"A wild animal might do this, rooting around," said Snap. "Could it have been a bear?"

"A bear!" ejaculated Giant. "Don't say a bear rooted around here while we were asleep! Why, it's enough to give a fellow heart failure thinking about it!"

"Wonder what time it is?" said the doctor's son, and felt for his watch. "Why, I declare, my watch is gone!" he exclaimed in consternation.

Just then Snap saw something on the ground and picked it up. It was a shred of a red bandanna handkerchief.

"Boys, do you know what I think?" he said excitedly. "I think our visitor was that wild hermit who lived in the lonely cabin in the woods!"

"You mean the one Whopper and I met?" asked Shep.

"Yes."

CHAPTER XVIII

A FIGHT WITH TWO WILDCATS

The doctor's son and Giant listened with interest to what their chum had to say.

"What makes you think it was the hermit?" asked Shep.

"Because of this bit of red handkerchief. Whopper said he saw such a bandanna around the wild man's neck or head."

"Gracious! so we did!" cried the doctor's son. "I had forgotten about it. But do you think that wild creature took my watch?" he added anxiously.

"Yes, unless you lost it on the way here."

"I didn't lose it before I went to sleep, for I wound it up, same as I do every night before retiring."

"Let us take a look around for it," suggested Giant.

A keen search was made, but nothing that looked like a watch could be located anywhere. Then, as they were a bit cold, the boys renewed the fire, thus adding to the light.

"If that wild man, or whatever he is, took my watch I want it back," declared the doctor's son.

"Do you think he'd take it to that cabin in the woods with him?" questioned Giant.

"More than likely."

"That must be a good way from here."

"It is. But you would want the watch if it was yours."

"Of course."

The boys talked the matter over for a quarter of an hour and then laid down to sleep once more, leaving the camp fire burning brightly. But the doctor's son could not slumber soundly, for his thoughts were on his missing timepiece, which had been a present and a valuable one.

They were up at sunrise, and then another consultation was had.

"I'd like to look for the watch," said Snap. "But if we don't get back to camp Whopper and Tommy will worry about us—and there is no telling what the Spink crowd will do in our absence."

"I suppose if that hermit has it the watch will be safe for a day or two," answered the doctor's son thoughtfully. "We might go back to the camp first and then make a trip to the cabin in the woods."

So it was decided, and after a hasty breakfast they set off in the direction of the Windy Mountains. They took the same trail as before, and on the walk kept their eyes open for game. They managed to bring down two grouse and a squirrel, but that was all. They reached camp an hour after sundown, much to the satisfaction of Whopper and Tommy, who came to meet them.

"Gosh! but I am tired!" said Snap as he threw his burden on

the ground. "I feel as if I wanted to rest for a week!"

"A good night's sleep will make you change your mind," answered the doctor's son.

Supper was ready for them, and they sat down gladly and partook of the things provided. During the day, to pass the time, Whopper and Tommy had baked a big pan of beans and another of biscuits, and both were good. They had also tried their hand at baking some cake, but this was a little burned. Yet the boys ate it and declared it was all right. At home it might have been different, but when one is out in the woods, and doing one's own cooking—well, there is no use in finding fault, that's all.

Whopper and Tommy listened with interest to what the others had to tell about the Spink crowd and about the midnight visitor. They laughed heartily over what had been done to the rowboat, and were serious over the loss of Shep's watch.

"I'd be afraid to meet that wild man," said Tommy. "Why, there is no telling what he would do if he was cornered."

"That is true," answered Shep. "Of course we can take our guns, but I'd hate to shoot anybody, even if it seemed necessary."

"Maybe he'll give in if we point our guns at him," suggested Whopper. "But I hardly think so. He may be as crazy as they make 'em and afraid of nothing."

"Well, I'll think it over," answered the doctor's son thoughtfully. He did not wish to expose his chums to danger, nor did he wish to get into trouble himself. Yet he felt the loss of the timepiece keenly.

The young hunters looked for a visit from the Spink crowd the next day, but it did not come. Instead, it rained, and they had to keep in the tent most of the time. But it cleared during the night, and the days to follow were ideal.

Sunday passed, and on Monday Shep, Snap and Whopper went out on a hunt, leaving Giant and Tommy in charge of the camp. Giant declared he was going to take and develop some photographs, using a daylight tank instead of a dark room for the latter process. It had been decided that some of the party should visit the lonely cabin in the woods later in the week.

The boys had seen some traces of wild beasts up the mountain side, and thither they directed their steps, keeping their eyes and ears on the alert as they proceeded. They had scarcely covered a quarter of a mile when they came upon the mutilated remains of a mink.

"Hello! what do you make of this?" cried Snap as he pointed it out.

"A mink, and some other wild beast killed it," said Whopper.

"Do you suppose it was a bear?" asked Snap.

"No; most likely a wildcat, or a big fox or wolf."

"Let's go after 'em!"

"They are no good for game—and that is what we are after."

"We might get some good photographs."

"That's so—I never thought of that!"

Filled with the idea of taking some pictures that might prove of value, the boys hurried on through the woods and up the side of the mountain. Shep cautioned the others to move as silently as possible, so hardly a word was said.

It was almost noon when they came to a flat spot, where there was something of a clearing. Here there was a spring and a pool, and a fallen tree lay across both.

"Wait!" whispered the doctor's son. "I think I see something!"

The others halted, and Shep advanced with increased caution, bringing his camera to the front as he did so.

The next instant he saw a sight that filled him with interest and pleasure. On the fallen tree spanning the pool rested two wildcats, mates, facing each other. Both had their eyes closed and were evidently asleep.

He motioned for the others to come up, and in a few seconds all were ready to take pictures. The background was perfect, and they felt this would be one of the finest subjects yet obtained.

Hardly daring to breathe, one after another of the boys clicked the shutter of his camera and the negatives were taken. Then they swung their cameras back and brought forward their shotguns.

As they did this one of the wildcats suddenly opened its eyes and looked around. On the instant it let out a cry of rage and its back commenced to bristle. Then the other wildcat leaped from the tree to the ground and crouched as if for a spring.

"Fire!" came the command from the doctor's son, but this was not necessary, for both Snap and Whopper blazed away as quickly as they could. The wildcat on the tree was hit and fell over into the pool with a loud splash. The other wildcat made a leap for Snap and hit him in the shoulder.

"Shoot him! shoot him!" yelled Snap in terror, and did what he could to keep the beast from reaching his breast and throat.

"Can't shoot—might hit you!" answered the doctor's son, but then he came up on the side and blazed away at close quarters, hitting the wildcat in the left hind leg. This caused the animal to drop to the ground, where it twisted and turned so quickly that the eyes of the young hunters could scarcely follow it.

The other wildcat had by this time climbed out of the pool. It gave itself a vigorous shake and turned as if to limp away. But then it espied its mate and stopped, as if calculating on what to do next.

"Shoot 'em!" sang out Whopper, and discharged his gun a second time. He hit the second wildcat in the back, but the wounds were not serious and the beast still thrashed around, snapping and snarling in a fashion that would have frightened any hunter.

The shot from the gun awakened the fury of the first wildcat, and crouching low it came toward Whopper step by step, its two eyes glowing like tiny electric lights. Whopper tried to run, but he was fascinated by the sight and too much overcome to move a step.

"Look out, Whopper!" screamed Snap, and then he raised his own gun to take another shot. But the hammer merely clicked. He tried it again, in increased haste, and as a consequence shot wild, the charge going over the wildcat's head.

Then the wildcat made a leap, striking Whopper and hurling him over backward. As he went down the second wildcat lurched itself forward, and in a twinkling both were on the young hunter, snapping and snarling as though about to eat him up!

CHAPTER XIX

SOME UNLOOKED-FOR GAME

It was a moment of dire peril and no one realized it more than did the young hunter who had been attacked by the two wild beasts of the forest. Like a flash he rolled over and doubled up to prevent the wildcats from reaching his head and neck.

This quick movement sent the animals to the ground, and as they landed Snap jumped forward and struck one of the wildcats with the stock of his gun. It was a telling blow, for by luck more than judgment it crushed the beast's skull.

The attack on its mate caused the other wildcat to pause. Then, filled with a sudden fear, and failing to get at Whopper's throat, it commenced to retreat.

"It's running away!" shouted Snap. "Kill it, Shep!"

The doctor's son had been dancing around, trying to get in a shot without injuring Whopper.

Now he leveled his shotgun and banged away. It was a close-range hit, and the head of the wildcat was almost blown from the body.

It was several seconds before the three boy hunters realized that the battle was at an end. Slowly Whopper turned over and looked at the two dead animals. He rose to his feet,

Captain Ralph Bonehill

panting heavily.

"Are they bo—both dead?" he asked.

"As dead as nails," answered Snap.

"I thought I was—was going to be—be chewed up!"

"It was a narrow escape."

"Say, after this, do you know what I think? I think we had better kill the beasts first and take the pictures afterward!"

"Then we'll not have such good photos," returned the doctor's son.

"Yes; but what good are photos to a fellow if he gets killed?" questioned Whopper ruefully.

"We'll have to be more careful, that's all," said Snap.

"What shall we do with the wildcats?"

"Leave them here, for all I care," answered the doctor's son. "The skins are not much good at this time of year and after such handling."

The three boys rested for a while, and then took a picture of the dead wildcats with themselves in the background. So that all might get in the pictures they set their cameras on rocks and worked them by means of threads of black linen.

"I am afraid our shots have scared away all the game in this vicinity," remarked the doctor's son as they, trudged forward once more. And so it seemed, for nothing came into view for the next hour. Then Snap sighted some rabbits, but before he could get a shot the game was out of sight.

At noon they rested in a glade that commanded a fine view of the surrounding country and each of the boys took several time pictures with small lens openings, so as to get sharp outlines.

It was well on toward the middle of the afternoon when they came upon the trail of a deer. It looked to be quite fresh, and this filled them with the hope of catching up to the game.

"We want to be mighty quiet," cautioned Snap, who was in the lead. "The wind is uncertain and may carry the slightest sound to the deer."

"It will carry our scent, too," answered Whopper.

"That we can't help and will have to chance."

They followed the trail for fully half a mile, through something of a hollow between the mountains. Here they came on quite a pond, much to their surprise. The pond was filled with lilies and other flowers, and on one side was a series of rocks leading to quite a cliff.

"What a beautiful spot for a cabin!" cried Shep, forgetting all about the deer, for a moment.

"Why not take some pictures?" suggested Snap. "We may not come this way again."

The doctor's son was willing, and they took several views, one of Whopper with his hand full of water lilies.

The trail of the deer led around the rocky elevation, and the three young hunters were moving through some low brushwood when of a sudden they heard a noise ahead of them.

"What's that?" asked Whopper.

"Bless me if I know," whispered the doctor's son. "Get your guns ready."

"Here comes a deer!" shouted Snap, and an instant later a magnificent buck burst into view, rushing around the other end of the cliff. It appeared and disappeared so quickly that to get a shot was all but impossible.

"Well, of all the chumps!" cried Snap in disgust. "Why didn't somebody let drive?"

"Why didn't you?" asked Shep.

"I couldn't—the rocks were in the way."

"Well, the rocks were in my way, too."

"How can a fellow shoot at a streak of greased lightning?" asked Whopper. "That buck was making a hundred miles a minute!"

"Well, that's the end of that game," muttered Snap, much crestfallen. "Boys, it looks as if we were going to be skunked to-day."

"Oh, we've got a couple of hours yet," said the doctor's son. "But I guess we had better turn back toward camp. We don't want to miss our way in the dark."

"Let us go on a little," said Whopper. "I imagine that buck got scared at something, and I'd like to know what it was."

"Maybe a bear," said Snap. "And if it is, you can be sure Mr. Bruin will walk right away from us while we are thinking about a shot," he added bitterly. He was disgusted to think they had allowed both the rabbits and the deer to get away from them.

All of the boys were curious to know if anything had really frightened the buck, and they went forward, but this time more cautiously than ever. Passing the cliff, they came to a hillside, overgrown with cedars and brushwood, with many loose stones between. Here they had to progress even more slowly, for walking was treacherous and none of them had a desire to twist an ankle or break a leg.

"I don't see a thing," said the doctor's son presently. "It's a mighty lonely place, isn't it?"

"I fancied I saw something move, just beyond yonder clump of cedars," said Whopper, pointing with his hand.

"Whopper is seeing things," said Snap, laughing. "I guess the wildcats and the deer got on his nerves."

"Well, don't believe me if you don't want to," answered Whopper rather testily.

"We'll see if there is anything in it, anyway," answered the doctor's son. "But I am not going any farther than those cedars. I am getting tired—and it is high time we turned back, unless we want to remain away from camp all night."

"No, I want to get back, too," answered Snap. "Sleeping out of doors is all well enough once in a while, but I prefer to be under some kind of a roof, even if it's only canvas."

The three boys moved forward once again, each with his gun ready for use, should anything worth shooting appear. They came up to the cedars and were then able to look beyond, where the mountain side was full of rocks, with numerous holes between.

"Oh!" yelled Snap at the top of his lungs. "Look!"

All gazed in the direction indicated, and for once they were fairly rooted to the spot. Before them, on a flat rock, stood a large and magnificent lion, gazing boldly at them.

CHAPTER XX

ON THE MOUNTAIN SIDE

For fully ten seconds the lion did not move, and during that time the young hunters stood spellbound. Then the foreign monarch of the forest turned and like a flash disappeared into a hole on the mountain side.

"Did—did—was it really a lion?" gasped Whopper when he could speak.

"It certainly was—and a big one, too," answered the doctor's son.

"But here?" began Snap. "We don't have lions in America."

"It must be the one that got away from the circus!" cried Shep.

"To be sure! Why didn't I think of that?" came from Whopper. "Sure as you're a foot high that is the circus lion. But how did he get away out here?"

"That's easy to explain," answered the doctor's son. "He left town and took to the woods, and his quest for food brought him here."

"And it was the lion that scared the buck," said Snap.

"More than likely. And he scared us, too. Why didn't you

shoot at him?"

"Why didn't you?"

"I guess we were all about paralyzed; I know I was," declared Whopper. "I didn't come out to hunt lions! Ugh! Maybe we had better get away from here. You can't kill a lion with a shotgun—you need a rifle, and a heavy one at that."

"Three heavy charges of buckshot would discourage any lion, I think," answered Shep. "At the same time, we don't want to run the risk of being torn to pieces by such a beast."

"Boys, I've got an idea!" cried Snap suddenly. "Maybe it won't work out, but we might try it."

"To kill the lion?"

"No, to capture him alive, and turn him over to the circus folks for that reward."

"What is the idea?"

"Let us dig a big pit here among the rocks and bait it with the two dead wildcats. We can drag the wildcats on the ground around here and to the pit, and maybe the lion will follow the trail up and fall into the pit."

"He'll be very obliging if he does that," said Whopper with a laugh. "I guess lions are as cautious as any wild beasts."

"He'll follow the trail if he gets hungry enough," said the doctor's son. "I think the idea is a good one, and I vote we follow it out at once.

"But to dig a pit will be lots of work," said Whopper. "Can't we find some ready-made hole that will do?"

Retreating still farther, and keeping their eyes and ears wide

Captain Ralph Bonehill

open for the possible reappearance of the monarch of the forest, the three young hunters at length found a hole that suited them. The bottom was filled with loose stones and decayed leaves, but these they soon cleaned out. Then, while Whopper went off for the dead wildcats, Snap and Shep made the hole still deeper. They removed the stones until they came to something of a small cave, and had to take care, for fear of tumbling in.

"I think that will hold the lion, if he deigns to come this way," said the doctor's son.

Over the top of the opening they placed some light brushwood, that would easily sink with the weight of any big beast, and in the center placed one of the dead wildcats. The other they dragged in a circle around the hole, and then let it fall to the bottom.

"That will give the beast something to eat, in case he is captured," said the doctor's son. "We don't want him to starve on our hands."

"I've got another idea," said Snap. "Why not fix one of the cameras so it will go off and take a picture, in case the lion touches a certain string? Mr. Jally told me how it could be done."

"A good idea!" cried Shep. "We'll do it right away. Only we don't want any flashlight, for that would scare the lion away."

"No; we'll have to run the risk of having the camera worked in the daylight."

It was dark by the time their task was accomplished. They knew that they could not get back to camp, yet none of them had any desire to remain in the vicinity of the lion.

"He might take it into his head to eat us up instead of the wildcats," said Whopper earnestly.

"Right you are," responded Shep. "We'll get as far away as we can."

They tramped for at least two miles, and during that time passed a mountain brook that was strange to them. They tried to get some fish, but were unsuccessful.

"We are skunked, and no mistake," said Snap dolefully. "Not even one fish or a rabbit for supper!"

"I am going to beat around the trees for something," said the doctor's son. "Shoot at anything that flies."

He walked ahead, and the others kept their guns in readiness. But all he stirred up were a few small birds not worth laying low.

"Lucky we saved a little of the grub," said Whopper. "If we hadn't we'd go to bed supperless."

"I am going to roost in a tree to-night, to keep out of the reach of that lion," said Snap.

All agreed that this would be a good thing to do, and after dividing what remained of the food brought along, and getting a drink at a spring, they selected a tree that suited their purpose and mounted to the thickest of the limbs.

"Not a very comfortable bed," was Shep's comment. "But better than falling into that lion's clutches."

"Shall we go back to the pit in the morning?" asked Whopper.

"No; let us go to camp first, and see how Giant and Tommy are making out," said the doctor's son. "Most likely they'll be worrying about us."

To keep from falling, the three young hunters tied themselves fast in the tree. They tried to sleep, but this was almost impossible, and the most each got were fitful naps, with many dreams of the lion. All thoughts of other game were, for the time being, banished from their minds.

At daybreak they descended to the ground and started for camp without waiting to shoot something for breakfast. They calculated they could get back before noon, and then they would eat a big dinner at their leisure.

All thought they had the "lay of the land" well fixed in their minds, and so they did not advance with the caution they might otherwise have taken. As a consequence, they presently made a false turn, and this brought them to a part of the mountains that was exceedingly rocky and rough.

"Say, we can't get through here," declared Whopper at last. "Why, it's worse than the Rocky Road to Dublin!"

"I believe we are off the right trail," returned Snap. "It seems to me our camp must be in that direction," and he pointed to their left.

"Perhaps you are right," said the doctor's son. "Anyway, we can't get through here. We'll ruin our shoes and run the risk of breaking our necks."

"Let us walk to the left," said Snap, and they turned back a short distance. As they did this, they started up a number of rabbits and, eager for some game, each blazed away, and as a consequence two of the creatures were brought low.

"Not much, but something," said the doctor's son.

They pressed on, soon coming to some rocks that were quite smooth.

"Be careful here," cautioned Snap. "A tumble would be a nasty thing. There is a cliff just below us."

He and the doctor's son went ahead and Whopper followed. The rocks were even more slippery than they had anticipated. The doctor's son was about to advise going back and walking around the cliff, when Whopper called out:

"A deer! I see a deer!"

"Where?" asked the others in a breath.

"Over yonder! I am going to give him a shot!"

In great excitement Whopper stood upright on the smooth rocks, raised his shotgun and pulled the trigger. But the deer was not hit, and a moment later disappeared from view.

The report of the shotgun was followed by a yell from Whopper. The weapon, had kicked back and sent him sprawling. Now he was rolling over and over on the smooth rocks, directly toward the dangerous cliff below him.

CHAPTER XXI

ADRIFT IN THE WOODS

"Stop Whopper, or he'll go over the cliff!"

It was the doctor's son who uttered the words. He was high up on the rocks and could do nothing to save his chum.

Snap heard and understood, for he saw Whopper rolling rapidly toward the cliff. If the youth went over, a sheer drop of twenty or thirty feet awaited him—with more rocks below.

In this moment of peril, for Snap to think was to Whopper was very dear to him, and he resolved to do all he could to save his chum, even at the risk of his own life.

He let his gun drop and ran over the rocks to where Whopper was rolling over and over. Then he caught him by the foot and threw himself flat, clutching tenaciously at a single stone that arose sharply above those around it. Snap's grip was good, and for the moment Whopper's progress was stayed.

"Don't move!" called out Snap as soon as he could catch his breath. "Press down on the rocks for all you are worth!"

Whopper understood and pressed down, and thus both boys lay quiet for several seconds. Whopper was but three feet from the edge of the cliff and Snap was just above him. The doctor's son was to the right, in a spot that was a comparatively safe one.

"The—the gun kicked!" gasped Whopper when he could speak.

"Yes, I know," answered Snap. "But be careful, or you'll go over the cliff yet!"

Whopper screwed his head around and gazed in the direction of the yawning gulf below him, and his face changed color.

"Gosh! We'll have to get out of this," he murmured.

"Crawl toward Shep; but take it slowly and be careful," directed Snap. "Shall I help you?"

"No, I can do it alone," was the answer.

Both boys crawled like snails over the smooth rocks until they gained the spot where the doctor's son rested. Whopper drew a long breath of relief.

"I'm glad I didn't take that tumble," he whispered hoarsely. He could hardly speak, and his limbs trembled slightly.

"It was a good thing Snap stopped you," said Shep.

"That's what—and I am mighty thankful, Snap," replied Whopper gratefully.

"Well, we'll have to go back, that is all there is to it," remarked the doctor's son after a pause, during which they looked across the rocks in perplexity. "I thought sure we could go this way, but it seems as if we can't."

To climb down the rocks was as great a task as it had been to climb up, and by the time they reached the bottom all were thoroughly hungry. It now lacked but an hour and a half of noon.

"We'll never get to camp by dinner-time," declared Snap. "And I'm not going to do without breakfast and dinner, too. I move we light a fire and cook those rabbits. I've got a little coffee left, enough for three weak cups, I guess."

The others agreed, and reaching a comfortable spot, they cut a little wood and made a fire. Then they sat down to rest while the skinned and cleaned rabbits were broiling. Snap made the coffee and, though rather weak and without milk and sugar, they drank it eagerly. They had a little salt for the rabbits, but that was all. But hunger and fresh air are great appetizers.

The scant meal at an end, they resumed their journey, the doctor's son taking the lead. They moved in a semicircle around the base of one small mountain and then reached a rather broad mountain torrent.

"Hello, here's a surprise!" cried Snap. "I had no idea such a big brook flowed through these parts."

"Nor I," added Shep. "Looks as if there might be good fishing here."

The boys noted the location of the brook, so that they might visit it another day, and then pushed on as before. They reached a slight rise and all concluded that their camp was directly to the west.

"In that case all we'll have to do is to follow the sun," declared Whopper.

"Right you are," responded the doctor's son.

"How far do you calculate it is?"

"Not more than two miles."

"It may be a little more," said Snap. "But not much."

They plunged into the woods once more, and had hardly proceeded a hundred yards when they heard some partridges drumming. It was a chance for another shot, and they hurried forward with guns ready for use.

"I see them!" cried Snap, and blazed away, and the others followed suit. They were unusually lucky, for five of the birds fell, either dead or fatally wounded. Soon they had the game in their bags.

"There! that is something like!" cried Snap. "They'll make fine eating." And he smacked his lips. He loved partridge meat very much.

They seemed to be getting deeper and deeper into the woods. The trees around them were so dense that it was almost impossible to see the direction of the sun. Several times they came to a halt to look around.

"What do you make of it?" asked Snap.

"I don't like it," answered the doctor's son emphatically. "First thing we know we'll be lost."

"Just what I was thinking."

"We were to follow the sun," came from Whopper.

"Can you see it?"

"Once in a while, and not very clearly at that."

"Tell you what we might do," suggested Shep. "Climb a big tree and take a look around."

This was considered a wise suggestion, and they started to carry it out. A tree was selected, and the others gave Snap a boost to the lower branches. Then up went the youth to the top, slowly but surely.

"Well, what do you see?" demanded the doctor's son, after having given his chum a chance to look around.

"Nothing."

"Nothing?" echoed Whopper blankly.

"Nothing but woods and mountains, and a brook or two. I don't see a thing that looks like a camp anywhere."

"Oh, it must be ahead of us," insisted the doctor's son.

"All right—you come up and locate it," grumbled Snap.

Shep came up and so did Whopper, and all three of the lads gazed longingly, first in one direction and then in another. Nothing but what Snap had mentioned greeted their eyes.

"Boys, we are lost!" cried Whopper.

"Oh, no, we're not lost—we are here," answered Snap. "The camp is lost."

"It's the same thing—so far as we are concerned."

"I think that is Firefly Lake," said Shep, pointing to a hazy spot in the distance. "And if it is, then our camp may lay around on the upper side of this mountain."

"That may be true."

"Shall we try to walk it?"

"Might as well, Shep. We don't want to stay here all night."

"And we don't want to walk two or three miles out of our way," put in Whopper. "I'm getting mighty tired—not having had a good rest last night."

"We are having one adventure on top of the other," said the doctor's son with a grim smile. "Well, is it go forward or stay here?"

Nobody wanted to stand still, and so they descended to the ground and moved off in the new direction settled upon. All were fagged out, so progress was slow. They encountered some squirrels and Snap brought down two and stowed them away with his partridge.

"There's a cat!" cried Shep suddenly, and ran forward. Then of a sudden he stopped and smiled, while Whopper and Snap roared.

"Better give that cat a wide berth," suggested Snap, "unless you want to put a whole perfumery shop to shame." And they did give the animal a wide berth, for it was a skunk, and one "ready for business," as Snap afterward expressed it.

By nightfall they were still deep in the woods. All were now exhausted, and coming to a fallen tree Snap dropped to rest and so did his chums.

"Boys, we have missed it," said the doctor's son seriously. "I must confess I haven't the least idea where our camp is!"

"And that means we'll have to stay out in these woods all night," returned Whopper.

"More than likely."

CHAPTER XXII

THE SPINK CROWD AGAIN

The prospect was not a pleasant one for the three boy hunters. It was not that they were afraid over the fact that they were lost in the woods on the mountain side. But they knew that Giant and Tommy would be greatly worried over their absence, and it was possible, yes, probable, that the two lads might have trouble with Ham Spink and his cronies.

"Ham will be as mad as a hornet if he had much trouble finding his boat," said Snap, in talking the situation over. "And the first thing he'll think of will be to get square."

"Well, if we can't get back we can't get back, and that is all there is to it," answered the doctor's son philosophically. "We've got to make the best of it."

"And then that lion—" added Whopper. But to this the others merely shrugged their shoulders.

They found a spot that seemed as good as any, and collecting some dry sticks built a camp fire and made themselves a supper. They were footsore and weary and glad to rest. Inside of an hour after eating all of the lads fell asleep, and each slept soundly until morning.

Snap was the first to awaken, and, letting the others rest, he replenished the camp fire and got breakfast ready. There was a sameness about their food that was not very appetizing, but this could not be helped.

"When I get back I'm going to live a whole day on pancakes and beans and bacon," said Whopper. "No more rabbits for me, or partridge, either."

"That's the one drawback to camping out," returned the doctor's son. "One does get awfully tired of eating game."

It was again a question of how to proceed, and once more they mounted a tree to take observations. They now saw two columns of smoke arising on the air, not a great distance off.

"Our camp fire and that of the Spink crowd!" exclaimed Snap. "I'll wager a button on it."

"I believe you are right," answered Shep. "We'll make for the nearest of 'em, anyway."

They set off at a brisk pace, taking as direct a route as the nature of the ground permitted. On the way they came to a large patch of huckleberry bushes and found the berries ripe and luscious.

"Let's pick some," said Whopper. "Then we can make huckleberry dumplings, or something like that."

"What about huckleberry pie?" suggested Snap.

"Great!"

They stopped long enough to pick several quarts of the berries, stowing the fruit away in one of the cleaned-out game bags. Then on they went as before.

Soon they broke through the woods into a clearing, and on the opposite side of this saw a camp, with several boys lolling around a camp fire. They were members of the Spink crowd and included Dick Bush and Carl Dudder.

"Say, where did you come from?" demanded Carl Dudder as he espied them and leaped to his feet.

"From the woods," answered Shep calmly.

"What do you want?"

"Nothing, Dudder, excepting to pass."

"Huh! You needn't look so innocent-like, Shep Reed! We know what you did to our boat," put in Dick Bush.

"What did we do to it?" asked Whopper.

"You know well enough. Think you're smart, don't you?" growled Carl.

"We know what you were going to do to our boat," put in Snap.

"What?"

"You heard what I said. We only got ahead of you, that's all."

"We'll fix you for it, don't you worry," said Carl with a cunning leer.

"Take care that you don't get into trouble," was Shep's answer. Then he walked around the camp fire and his chums followed.

"Where are you going?" asked one of the other members of the Spink crowd.

"That is our business."

At this answer the other lads merely scowled. There was an awkward pause, and then Shep and his chums moved on and plunged into the woods beyond the camp fire.

"They are a real sociable bunch," was Whopper's sarcastic comment. "How I would love to stay with them!"

"I'll wager they fight like cats and dogs," put in the doctor's son. "I don't believe they have one real pleasant day." And he was right; the Spink crowd were usually wrangling from morn to night and already one of the number had left and started for home in disgust.

The boy hunters had the best part of half a mile farther to go, but this they soon covered and then came to an opening that looked familiar to them. Close at hand was their own camp. As they approached they heard loud talking.

"You clear out, Ham Spink, and leave us alone," came in the voice of Giant. "We don't want you around here. And we don't want you, either, Ike Akley."

"We'll leave when we please," was the answer from Ham Spink.

"We aren't going to hurt you," said the boy named Ike Akley, another of the Spink contingent.

"We don't want you around."

"Got anything good to eat?" demanded Ham coolly.

"Not for you."

"We'll not go until you give us something good."

"That's the talk!" cried Akley.

Let's take a look around and see if we can find any cookies!" said Ham.

"You leave our things alone," said Giant firmly.

"Bah! You fellows didn't leave our boat alone, so why should we leave your things alone?" growled Ham.

"I won't have you looking through our things," cried Giant.

He stepped up in front of Ham, who was much taller and heavier. At the same time Tommy ran to a distance and picked up two good-sized stones.

"You touch him or the things and I'll throw these!" cried the boy from the circus. "And I'll set my dog on you, too!"

"You little rat, you!" roared Ham. "Don't you dare to interfere with me."

"I'll take care of the kid!" cried Ike Akley, and strode toward Tommy. But in a twinkling the boy from the circus had leaped into a tree and was safe among the branches. The stones he had put in his pockets, but now he brought them forth again.

"Just remember what I said!" he exclaimed. "I'm a good shot, too!"

"We'll get the best of 'em, and take what we please!" cried Ham Spink.

"Will you?" called out Shep, advancing into the opening, with his gun in his hands. "I rather guess not."

Ham looked around, and so did Ike Akley. When both saw the doctor's son, Snap and Whopper, and all with their guns in their hands, they fell back and grew a trifle pale.

"Thought you were going to rob us, eh?" said Shep sternly.

"N—no," stammered Ham. "We—er—we were only going to take a—er—cookie or two, if you had 'em."

"Well, you'll not take a thing, so clear out!"

"You—you took our boat," said Ham.

"And you were going to take ours, only you didn't find it," said Snap with a grin.

"You hadn't any right to touch our boat."

"See here, Ham, don't talk like a child. After all you did to harm us in the past we've got a right to do almost anything to you, and you know it," said the doctor's son. "Now you clear out and leave us alone."

"You've been following us," put in Ike Akley.

"Not at all."

"Then why did you come away out here to camp?"

"Because we chose to come. Now, clear out—and stay away!"

A wordy war lasting several minutes followed. It was plainly to be seen that the shifting of the boat had filled Ham Spink with rage, and he was unusually anxious to "square up" with the four boy hunters. But he could do nothing, and at last he and his crony withdrew.

"I am glad you arrived," said Giant. "If you hadn't I am afraid those fellows would have gotten the best of us."

"I would have shied rocks at them," said Tommy, who had come down from the tree. "They may be bigger than I am, but I guess I could outrun 'em," and at this remark the others had to smile.

"More than likely they'll come back some time," said Snap. "And they'll bring the others with them. We'll have to remain on guard. But, Tommy, I've got great news."

"What is that?"

"We've spotted a lion—the one that got away from the circus."

"A lion!" ejaculated Giant.

"Yes; and we are hoping to trap the beast and get the reward offered for its return," said Whopper.

CHAPTER XXIII

A BEAR AND A LION

Giant and Tommy listened with interest to what the others had to tell about the wildcats, the deer and the lion, and also about the stop at the Spink camp. The story about the lion interested Tommy deeply.

"Casso will be glad to get that lion back," he said. "And if you capture him alive he ought to be willing to pay well for it."

Giant and Tommy had had a rather quiet time in camp. They had hunted and fished a little, and Giant had taken some photos and developed some films and plates and printed a few pictures. The photographs had turned out well, and the young hunters were correspondingly proud of them.

"I think my father will be much pleased," said the doctor's son. "I am sure they are right in line with what he wanted. But we must get a good many more."

"How about your watch, Shep?" asked Whopper.

"I declare, I forgot about it—thinking of that lion," answered the doctor's son. "We'll have to go to that lonely cabin and see if I can't get it back from that crazy hermit—if he is around."

A day's rest seemed to make Snap and Shep feel as lively as ever, but Whopper declared that he was still tired out, and, besides, he had scraped an ankle on the rocks and this was quite sore. He said that he was willing to take it quiet for at least a day or two more.

"We'll have to see about that lion, and about that hermit," declared Shep. "Supposing we leave you and Tommy in camp this time, and take Giant along?"

"All right," said Whopper.

"Do you think you can manage—if the Spink tribe come to bother you?" asked Snap.

"I think so—unless they come at night."

"You'll have to risk that."

"Wags will watch out at night," said Tommy. "He's better as a watch dog at night than he is in the daytime."

It was decided that the boys should try first to find out if the lion had been trapped. Then they were to journey to the lonely cabin in the woods. Not knowing how long they would be away. They took with them a fair stock of provisions and also a good supply of matches. They also took new films and plates for their cameras. Fortunately, in spite of the rather rough experiences of the boys, none of the picture-taking machines had been damaged, beyond having the leather covers scratched, and this did not matter.

"They don't look so well," said Shep. "But they'll do the work, and that's what we want."

The doctor's son, with Snap and Giant, started early on the following morning. Giant was glad to get away from the camp once more, and whistled a merry tune as they hurried along. They cut around the Spink camp, not wishing to meet their enemies.

"No use of letting them know we are gone," said Snap. "If they did, they'd be sure to go and bother Whopper and Tommy at once—and two couldn't do much against that whole crowd."

Snap and Shep had fixed the direction well in their mind and studied the position of the sun, so that they might not go astray. Having left the Spink camp behind them, the three boys struck out in a bee line for the spot where they had left the pit with the dead wildcats as bait. They made good progress, and stopped less than half an hour for lunch at midday.

"We ought to reach there before nightfall," said the doctor's son. "That is, unless we get turned around again."

"I think we are going straight," answered Snap. "But it may be farther than you think."

While tramping along they scared up several rabbits, and Giant brought down one of these. But game appeared to be scarce and nothing else came to view.

It was just five o'clock when they reached a clearing that looked familiar to Snap and Shep.

"That pit is just beyond here," said the doctor's son. "We'd better go slow—in case that lion hasn't been caught and is at large."

The others took the advice and advanced with caution. A fringe of brushwood hid the pit from view. On the other side of the clearing was a dense forest of pines and hemlocks.

"Well, I never!"

It was the doctor's son who uttered the exclamation. He was slightly in advance and had peered over the bushes.

"What is it?" asked Snap in a low tone.

"Look, but don't make any noise."

Snap and Whopper pressed forward and looked. What they saw thrilled them greatly.

On the edge of the pit was a fair-sized black bear. He was sniffing at the carcass of the wildcat that rested on the tree branches laid over the mouth of the opening.

"A chance for a fine shot!" whispered Giant a bit nervously.

"Wait—we'll get a picture first!" said the doctor's son. "But keep quiet!"

The others understood, and, hardly daring to breathe, the three lads swung their cameras into position, got them ready for use, and spread out among the bushes to take some snapshots.

The bear was a cautious animal and slowly he circled the pit, sniffing longingly at the carcass so close at hand. Evidently he desired a meat diet for a change and wanted to get the wildcat very much, but did not quite trust the tree branches and what might be underneath.

Each of the lads got what he thought was a good picture, and then Snap and Giant looked at Shep and touched their guns. But the doctor's son did not see them, for he was looking wildly at something between the trees on the other side of the clearing.

"What do you see?" whispered Snap.

"Hush!" answered the doctor's son. "Look for yourself."

Snap and Giant gazed in the direction pointed out, and it must be confessed that the hair of the smaller youth literally rose on end. There, between two trees, crouched the lion that had escaped from the circus. The eyes of the monarch of the forest were fastened on the bear, and his tail was swaying from side to side, showing that he was getting ready for a leap.

"Shall we—we shoot?" asked Snap. He was so agitated he could hardly speak.

"Why not take a picture?" asked Shep, who had his camera still in his hand.

"All right—but we don't want that lion to—to come this way."

"Not much!" put in Giant, and it must be confessed that his voice trembled a good deal. To face a deer or even a bear was one thing; to face a powerful lion was quite another.

Slowly the lion came out from between the two trees. The bear now had his head turned the other way, so he was not aware of the approach of the enemy.

It made a magnificent picture, and for the moment the boys forgot their own peril and each took two snapshots, one with the lion almost on top of the bear.

Scarcely had they clicked the shutters of the cameras the second time when a blood-curdling roar rent the air, and the lion made one grand leap for the bear. But as this happened bruin chanced to turn slightly, and with a movement wonderful in such a bulky animal the bear sprang to one side. The lion missed his would-be prey and slid forward, directly into the mass of tree limbs covering the pit.

"He's going into the hole!" cried Snap. "Look!"

All gazed on the scene and saw that Snap was right. Unable to stop himself, the lion had crashed down between the tree limbs and was now struggling vainly to reach firm ground once more. The bear backed away and then, turning, sped off among the trees, not over a dozen yards from where the young

Captain Ralph Bonehill

hunters were in hiding.

"The bear—he's coming this way!" yelled Snap.

"Shoot him!" screamed Giant. And he brought around his gun.

All tried to get a shot, but the trees were too thick, and in a few seconds the bear was out of sight, crashing down the brushwood as he went.

He was badly frightened, and with good cause, for a lion was a new enemy for him.

As the bear disappeared the boy hunters turned their attention again to the lion. The monarch of the forest was doing his best to climb over the tree limbs, which turned and bent between him.

"Shall we shoot him?" queried Snap. "If he gets loose."

"There he goes!" shouted Shep.

As the doctor's son spoke they heard a tree limb snap in twain. For one instant the lion clung to the broken end, then, with a roar, the beast sank out of sight into the pit.

CHAPTER XXIV

A NOTABLE CAPTURE

"We've got him! We've got him!" shouted Snap, and his heart gave a wild bound of pleasure.

"Don't be too sure," cautioned the doctor's son. "Wait—keep your gun ready for use."

"That's it—he may get out of the pit," came from Giant. "Don't take any risks. He could kill a fellow in a minute, if he got the chance!"

They waited, each with his gun ready. Down in the pit they heard the lion growling and slashing around. Evidently he was doing his best to get out of the hole.

"I'll bet he's mad," said Snap.

"One of the dead wildcats is with him," said Snap. "That will give him something to eat."

"He'll not think of eating just now," answered the doctor's son. "He knows he is in a bad fix."

They waited a minute longer and then the lion became quiet. At last the three boy hunters ventured into the clearing and Shep, with his gun raised, walked slowly to the edge of the pit.

Suddenly a fearful roar rent the air, echoing far and wide across the mountains. The lion had discovered the doctor's son. His mane bristled and he showed his cruel teeth to the full.

"Can he—do you think he can get out?" asked Snap.

"Hardly, or he'd be out already," answered Shep. "Let us pull those branches away. They might give him some sort of a foothold."

All three of the boys came up and gazed down on the captured beast. They hauled the tree branches away and threw the second dead wildcat into the pit. Snap did this, and it seemed to cause the lion some surprise. He shut his mouth, his eyes began to blink, and presently he bent down and commenced to feed on one of the carcasses.

"He knows he is a prisoner," cried Snap. "See, he's acting just as if he was in the circus." For the monarch of the forest had laid down, with the meat between his heavy fore paws.

"I've got an idea," said Shep, looking around. "There are a great number of flat stones on the mountain side. Let us shove them down here and pile up a sort of wall around the top of the pit. That will surely keep the lion in."

This was considered a good suggestion, and all the lads set to work without delay. Some of the stones were so large it took two to lift them. They made an excellent wall, and inside of an hour the boys had a barrier around the top of the pit three feet high.

"I don't think he'll get out in a hurry," said Shep. "But to make sure we can cut some poles and lay them over the stones and pile more stones on top."

"Humph! Why didn't you mention the poles first?" said Snap.

"I didn't think of it, Snap."

The saplings were cut and placed in a row over the top of the pit and then some stones were put on top of these. Evidently the lion did not like to have his light and air cut off, and he commenced to roar again. But this the boys did not mind, for they now knew they had him fast.

It goes without saying that all the boys were delighted over their catch.

"We'll have to get word to the circus folks as quickly as possible," said Snap. "But where the show is now I don't know."

"Probably Tommy knows the route the circus was to take," answered the doctor's son.

"He does, for he spoke to me about it," put Giant. "But I have forgotten the towns and dates."

"Do you know what I'd like to do before going on to that lonely cabin?" went on Snap.

"What?"

"Go after that bear."

"Oh, he is probably miles away by this time," said the doctor's son. "He was too scared to stay around here."

"Well, let us go after him, anyway. He went in the direction of the cabin—that is, partly."

"Well, we'll see in the morning," said Shep.

The three boy hunters went into camp not very far away from the pit holding the lion. Once or twice they went up to view their precious prize, and noted that after eating one of the wildcats the lion stretched out and went to sleep.

"Guess he thinks he's back in the menagerie," said Giant. "Well, let him, if only he'll keep quiet until the circus people take him away."

It was such a warm night they did not bother with a camp fire, but eating some of the food brought along, soon retired and went sound asleep. Once Giant awoke with a start and imagined that the lion was after him, but he soon went to sleep again.

I'm the morning they found the captured lion still resting quietly on the bottom of the pit. He had not touched the second wildcat.

"He'll have plenty of food," said Snap. "But how about water?"

"I was thinking of that," answered the doctor's son. "We'll have to bring some from a spring and lower it to him."

They took the kettle they had brought along and filled it at a spring they had found and lowered this into the pit by means of a piece of fishingline Grant carried. At first the lion roared in rage, but when he saw the water he drank eagerly. They had to fill the kettle three times before he was satisfied. Then they took more water and poured it in a hollow on one side of the pit bottom.

"Now he won't go thirsty for a long time," said Shep.

They cooked themselves a good breakfast and a little later set off across the hills in the direction of the end of Firefly Lake. It was their purpose to get to the lake by noon if possible, and then strike out along the rocky watercourse leading to Lake Cameron.

"We'll have to be careful how we tackle that hermit," said the doctor's son. "He may be the craziest kind of a lunatic."

"I've got an idea," said Snap. "Wouldn't it be a good idea to wait until night and then crawl up to the cabin while he is asleep?"

"It may be—if he didn't take us for robbers and act worse than ever."

"Why not try him in the daytime first, and then, if you can't get the watch, go back at night?" said Giant.

"He may prowl around at night," suggested Shep. "And, remember, he may not have the watch at all—it's all guesswork."

It was an exceedingly warm day, and when it was near noon all three of the young hunters were glad enough to lie down in the shade and rest. Game appeared to be as scarce as the day before and all they shot were some rabbits and one squirrel.

"We've got to do better than this before we go home," said Shep.

"If we only knew what had become of that bear!" sighed Snap.

"Yes, if we only did!" murmured Giant.

It was so pleasant in the shade that none of the boys could get up ambition enough to go on until they had taken a nap. Then they went up a hill slowly, carrying their coats over their shoulders.

"If it's hot here, what must it be in town?" said the doctor's son.

"About ninety in the shade!" cried Snap.

At the top of the hill they took another rest. Here there was a little breeze, for which they were thankful.

"There is the lake!" cried Giant, pointing to a sheet of water below them. "One good thing, it will be easier going downhill than it was coming up."

"I vote we go in for a good swim when we reach the lake," said Snap. "What do you say, Shep?"

"I'd rather get to that cabin, before it is too late. But I'll take a ten-minutes' dip, if you wish."

So it was agreed, and the boys hurried through the woods to the lake shore in a pleasant frame of mind.

"Listen!" cried Snap presently. "What's that—a dog?"

All listened and heard a loud barking, coming from the neighborhood of the water.

"I think it's a fox!" cried Giant. "You'll remember, they bark just like that!"

"Let's try to get a photo and a shot!" answered the doctor's son. "Nothing like getting pictures of everything," he added.

They increased their speed, and soon found themselves within a hundred yards of the shore of Firefly Lake. The barking had now ceased, and they stood still, not knowing in which direction to turn.

"Something moving over yonder," whispered Giant presently, and nodded with his head down the lake shore.

Making no noise, they went forward again. They had to pass some bushes and rocks, and then came to a point where a spur of land jutted far out into Firefly Lake. It was a rocky and sandy spur, with scarcely any brushwood on it.

"There you are!" said Snap, and pointed to the extreme end of the spur. There, on the rocks, were two large foxes, their noses well in the air, gazing down the lake attentively.

"We've got them," murmured the doctor's son. "Come on, we'll take pictures first and then shoot them!"

He brought around his camera and the others did likewise. They had just snapped the shutters when the foxes turned, saw them, and set up a loud and angry barking and showed their teeth.

"They are coming for us!" yelled Giant, and he was right. Without hesitation, the foxes made several big leaps and came directly for the young hunters!

CHAPTER XXV

THE TWO FOXES

Ordinarily the foxes would have turned and run away, but, with the lake behind them, this was impossible, consequently they showed fight. They came on snapping and snarling viciously and with their teeth gleaming in a manner that made the boys shudder.

Fortunately for the young hunters the distance from the spur of rocks to where the lads stood was over fifty yards, so, as the foxes came rushing on, they had just time enough to shove aside their cameras and bring their shotguns to the front. Snap was the first of the three to bring his weapon into play, and he pulled the trigger when the fox was less than a dozen feet away.

The shot was a fairly good one, for it took the beast just under the breast. The fox gave a yelp of intense pain and dropped back.

The other fox came rushing at the doctor's son. The strap of Shep's gun had become entangled with that of his camera and consequently it was next to impossible for him to bring the weapon into proper play. He fired, but the charge went too high, and the beast continued to come on, until it crouched at his feet, snapping viciously and getting ready to leap at his throat.

It was now that Giant showed his mettle. He, too, had had a

little trouble in getting at his gun, but now the weapon was pointed at the fox at Shep's feet. Giant ran closer and pulled the trigger. Bang! went the gun, and the fox received the full charge directly in the left ear. It keeled over, and Giant sent the second charge of his double-barreled weapon into the second fox, and that, too, went down and lay quivering in its death agonies.

It took the young hunters some time to recover from the excitement of the occurrence. The attack of the foxes had come so quickly that it had startled them greatly.

"This ought to be a warning to us—this and that fight with the wildcats," said Snap. "We ought to be on our guard every minute. We've been lucky so far—maybe some other time we'll not do so well."

"Don't borrow trouble, Snap," answered the doctor's son. "Yet I agree with you, we must be more careful in the future. Is your camera all right?"

"I think so."

"Then let us take pictures of ourselves with the dead foxes," went on Shep, and this was done, and later the photographs turned out very well.

Having finished with the picture-taking, the boys threw off their clothing and went for a swim in the clear, cool waters of Firefly Lake.

"Say, this is fine!" cried Snap enthusiastically as he splashed the water around. "Makes a fellow feel a year younger, after such a hot tramp as we have had!"

"That's what!" answered the doctor's son. "Look at this!" he added as he made a long dive from a rock beside which he knew the water to be deep.

They dove and swam and splashed around to their hearts' content for a good quarter of an hour, and even had a little race to a snag sticking up from the bottom fifty yards from the rocks. Then Shep said they had better dress and proceed on their way.

They ran out of the lake, shook themselves, and made for the spot whe`e they had left their clothing behind some bushes. Each stared in amazement. The clothing had been left in three heaps; now the garments were strewn around in helter-skelter fashion.

"Somebody has been here!" cried Snap. "Is anything gone?" demanded Giant. At this all took a hasty inventory of their possessions.

"My shirt is missing!" came from the doctor's son.

"One of my socks is gone," added Giant.

"My belt is gone," came from Snap, "and so is my camera."

"And my gun!" added Shep, looking around to where the weapons had rested against a tree.

"Boys, we have been robbed!"

"What enemy has done this?"

"Can this be the work of the Spink crowd?"

For a minute the talk was lively, and then the boys calmed down a little. Even in their excitement they were glad that nothing more had been taken.

"I don't think the Spink crowd did this," said Snap. "Ham Spink wouldn't stop short of taking everything."

"Exactly my idea of it," answered Giant.

"Whoever it was had a queer idea of what to take," said the doctor's son slowly. "A shirt, a belt, one sock, a camera and a gun. Why in the name of goodness did he take one sock and not the other?"

"He certainly threw things around pretty well," said Giant. "Maybe it was a wild animal," he continued suddenly.

"No wild animal would walk off with a camera and a gun, Giant," returned Snap. "Ha! I have it!" he cried. "That crazy hermit!"

"Maybe you're right," said Shep. "It would be just like such a fellow to do a thing like this."

"And if he did this he must certainly have taken the watch," went on Snap.

"It would seem so."

The boys lost no time in dressing. As it was warm, Shep did not miss his shirt very much, nor did Giant miss his sock. Having no belt, Snap used a piece of stout cord instead.

"The loss of the gun is bad," said the doctor's son as they were finishing their toilet. "For if that crazy fellow has it, it will be so much harder to tackle him."

"That's true," answered Snap. "Maybe he'll shoot himself with it—if he's so very crazy."

"Oh, we'll not hope that," murmured Giant.

They took the dead foxes and hung them high up in a tree, intending, if possible, to come for them later and turn the meat over to the captured lion. Then they pushed forward in the direction of the rocky waterway that connected the two lakes.

"You'll have to lead," said Snap to the doctor's son. "You've been here before."

"I'll lead as well as I can," was the answer. "But there is no regular trail—that is, on the other side of the river."

The walking now became very rough, and the three young hunters had to proceed slowly. At times they were in sight of the water, but often their course led them inland for a hundred yards or more.

"These rocks are something fierce!" exclaimed Giant at length, after slipping and sliding several times.

"You beware that you don't twist an ankle," cautioned Snap.

Presently they reached a spot where further progress seemed impossible. Giant and Snap halted and looked at Shep.

Before them was a little hollow, filled with small stones, and beyond were some shelving rocks with large cracks between. Over the shelving rocks grew heavy masses of vines.

"Don't drag," urged the doctor's son. "It is getting late. The sun will be down in another hour."

"I can't go any faster," panted Giant. All three advanced and tried to climb the shelving rocks by holding on to the vines. Some of these gave way, and the three boys fell back. Then from under the rocks came a strange, hissing sound, followed by a curious rattle.

"What's that?" cried Snap.

"Snakes!" roared the doctor's son. "Back for your lives, fellows! We have struck a den of rattlesnakes!"

CHAPTER XXVI

MORE OF A MYSTERY

There was a wild scrambling on the part of all the young hunters to get out of the zone of danger. They leaped for the rocks behind them, and Shep and Snap succeeded in mounting to spots of comparative safety. But Giant was not so successful, and, slipping and sliding, He rolled over and over, coming to a stop when flat on his back.

"Get up! get up!" screamed the doctor's son. "Hurry up, Giant!"

Shep and Snap had caught sight of three rattlesnakes, that had glided from between the shelving rocks ahead. They were all of good size. One had been caught in the torn-away vines and was hissing viciously, and the other two were sounding their rattles, preparatory to striking at the smaller youth.

Giant did not remain upon his back long. The instant he landed he started to turn over. He saw one of the snakes draw near and make a strike at his sockless ankle. Giant let out a yell like an Indian on the warpath, and, on all fours, made a leap like a frog a distance of several feet. Then he stood upright and made another leap for the rocks. As he came close, Snap caught him by the arm and pulled him still higher.

The doctor's son was the only person capable, just then, of using a gun, and having no weapon of his own he grabbed

Snap's and blazed away. Whether he hit a snake or not he could not tell. There was a hissing and rustling among the torn away vines, and when the smoke of the discharge cleared away the snakes were no longer to be seen.

"Ugh! what—a—a thing t—to happen!" said Giant with a shiver. His emotion was so deep he could scarcely speak.

"Where are the snakes now?" asked Snap, and drew himself up on the highest rock he could find.

"I don't know—hiding, I suppose," answered the doctor's son as he peered around sharply for a sight of the reptiles.

The three boys waited for fully two minutes, not daring to make a move. The vines lay where they had been cast, and between them lay Giant's gun, which he had dropped when trying to leap to safety.

"I guess we had better get out of this locality," said Snap at length. "I have no desire to be bitten by a rattlesnake!"

"Indeed not!" answered Giant. "But my gun—I don't want to leave that behind."

"Do you want to go down for it?"

"Not for a thousand dollars!" answered the small youth vehemently. "Why, a rattlesnake bite is deadly poisonous!"

"I know that as well as you do, Giant."

"You might make a cast with your fishing-line," suggested the doctor's son.

"I will."

Giant always carried several lines, and selecting one of these, he made a loop and to it fastened a small sinker for a weight.

Then he made a cast for the gun and secured it.

Slowly and cautiously, and keeping on the highest rocks they could find, the three young hunters commenced to retreat. They moved back at least fifty yards, and then made a wide detour along the hill skirting the watercourse. All this took time, and when they thought themselves safe it was growing dark.

"This doesn't look as if we were going to get to the cabin very fast," remarked Snap. "How much farther have we to go?"

"A good half mile," answered Shep.

"Then we might as well go on, even if it is night," put in Giant. "Perhaps we can catch that crazy fellow asleep and make him a prisoner. He ought to be arrested for stealing our things."

Presently the doctor's son came to a spot that looked familiar, and a minute later he pointed to a notch cut in a tree.

"That is my blaze," he said. "I made it so as to remember where the cabin was located. We'll be there in a few minutes more. Better keep quiet."

The others understood, and after that they advanced without speaking, unless it seemed necessary, and then only in a whisper. The sun had gone down, and it was as quiet as it was lonely.

The doctor's son was in the lead, and presently he halted and pointed ahead. There was the dilapidated cabin, just as it had been when visited by Shep and Whopper.

"See anybody?" asked Giant in a low voice.

"Not a soul."

"Supposing we walk around the place first?" suggested Snap.

The others agreed to this, and they circled the lonely structure at a distance of twenty yards. Nobody appeared, nor did they hear any sound from within.

"I may be mistaken, but it looks deserted to me," said Snap.

"Well, we thought it was deserted, too, until that fellow shied things at us," answered the doctor's son.

At last, growing a bit bolder, the three lads walked slowly up to the cabin, Snap and Giant with their guns ready for use and the doctor's son with a stout stick he had cut. Thus they reached the doorway, which was wide open. Shep looked in, shielding his head with one arm, for he did not know but what he might become the target for anything the strange creature living there should have in hand.

The place was pitch dark inside, and for the moment the doctor's son could see nothing. But as his eyes grew accustomed to the gloom he saw a broken table and an old bench, and several discarded articles of culinary ware.

"Do yo—you se—see him?" whispered Giant. He was so agitated he could scarcely frame the words.

Shep shook his head, and, growing still bolder, stepped into the lonely cabin. With added caution his two chums followed. They tiptoed their way through the two rooms and back again.

"He must have gone out," said Snap at last.

"Shall I make a light?" And as the others assented he struck a match and lit the pocket lantern he had brought along.

The rays of the small light revealed a curious scene to them. In a corner, where it had been hurled, lay Shep's gun. It had been discharged and the buckshot had gone through one sleeve of the shirt that had been stolen and which likewise lay in the corner. There was some blood on the shirt, and bloodstains led across the floor to the doorway and outside.

"Must have shot himself," was Snap's comment.

"Yes; and ran away after he did it," returned Giant.

"See anything of my watch?" asked Shep.

"No; and I don't see my belt or my camera, either," answered Snap.

"Or my sock," put in Giant.

The inner room of the cabin was littered up with a variety of things, the wings of birds, feathers of chickens, shells of eggs, bones, bits of tree branches, an old iron chain, a tiny square looking-glass, badly cracked, some stale bread and cake, cores of apples and pears, and a great mass of other trash.

"He's a regular pig," was Snap's comment.

"Wonder if he'll come back to-night?" was Giant's question.

"Perhaps, unless he was fatally wounded," answered Shep.

They made a thorough search for the missing watch, camera, and other things, but without success. Shep would not touch the shirt, and left it where it was. But he took the gun, and after examining it proceeded to load up the empty barrel.

"We'll go into camp near here," said the doctor's son. "And keep watch for the missing person, whoever he is."

They got supper and went into camp close to the rear of the cabin. They took turns at watching throughout the entire night, but nothing came to disturb them. Early in the morning they visited the cabin again, but found nothing new to interest them. Coming out, Giant started up two rabbits and quickly shot the game.

"Say, that will bring him back, if he's in this vicinity," cried Snap. "Perhaps it would have been better—"

He stopped speaking, for as he spoke they heard another gunshot from the woods between them and the river. Then came a call that sounded somewhat familiar.

CHAPTER XXVII

AN OLD FRIEND APPEARS

"That can't be the wild man, can it?" queried Giant.

"No," answered the doctor's son. "I think I know that voice."

"I think it's Jed Sanborn," came from Snap.

They waited for a few minutes and then saw a familiar figure emerge from the woods. It was their old hunting friend, and in his hand he carried six partridges.

"Hello, there!" he cried on coming closer. "Thought you fellers was a-goin' up to the Windy Mountains?"

"We've been up—have our camp there," answered the doctor's son. "We came down here for a purpose."

"Everything all right at home?" asked Giant.

"Yes. We had a scare day before yesterday, though. Hicks' barn got afire, an' folks thought the town might burn down, account o' the wind. But the bucket brigade an' the engine got the fire out before anything else caught."

"Are our folks all well?" asked Snap.

"Yes; an' hopin' you are the same, as they write in letters,"

Captain Ralph Bonehill

and the old hunter grinned. "Had much luck shootin' and picter-takin'?"

"We are well satisfied," answered Shep. "Got quite some partridge and rabbits and some deer, and a lion—"

"Oh, sure! A lion! Suppose ye got an ellerphant, and hoppo-what-you-call-'em, too?"

"We did get a lion," said Giant. "We've got him in a pit."

"See here, son, lions don't roam these woods, an' never did. You are mistook in the beast."

"It's the circus lion, Jed; the one that got away at Railings," explained Snap.

"Oh! Do ye really mean it?" And now Jed Sanborn was tremendously interested.

"Yes. We saw him on the mountain side and found a big pit and made a trap of it with some wildcat meat, and we caught him."

"Is he alive an' well?"

"Yes."

"Glory to Washington! Do you know them circus folks has offered a reward o' three hundred dollars fer that lion if caught alive?"

"Then the money is ours!" cried Shep. "Hurrah, boys, that suits me down to the ground!"

"Are you sure about the reward?" asked Snap.

"O' course—I read the poster in the post-office. They'll give three hundred dollars fer the lion an' five hundred fer the eddicated chim—what-you-call-him. You know."

"The educated chimpanzee," said Shep.

"That's it. It looks as if that chimpanzee was wuth a lot to them. He was a whole show in hisself."

"Well, we've got the lion right enough," said Snap. "We don't know anything about the monkey."

They told the old hunter about many of their doings, and related the story of the missing watch, camera, and other things.

"Why, I didn't know anybody lived in this cabin," said Jed Sanborn. "It's been empty ever since old Sturgis died—about twelve years ago. He had some awful disease—like smallpox—and folks got scared to come here."

"Gracious! You don't suppose we'll get any disease?" cried Giant in alarm.

"Not from him, son—it's too long ago. Why, say, I was at this cabin less than a month ago—stopped here overnight account o' a rainstorm."

Wasn't nobuddy here then. It can't be Peter Peterson, can it?"

"No; it didn't look like Peterson," answered the doctor's son. "Besides, Peterson isn't so plumb crazy as this chap."

"I'll take a look around," answered Jed Sanborn.

He made the same investigation as had the boys. Then he got down on his hands and knees and examined the soft ground in and around the cabin.

"Say, did ye see anything o' a dog around here?" he asked.

"Yes," answered Giant. "That is, the circus boy we told you about has his dog with him—a collie."

"Here's a trail looks something like a dog's, but not much. Plenty o' other footmarks—but I reckon you made those."

What to do next the boys did not know. There was no telling what had become of the strange occupant of the lonely cabin, or when he would return.

"We'd like to let those circus folks know about the lion," said the doctor's son. "I suppose one of us will have to go back to town to send them word."

"I am going back to town to-morrow," answered the old hunter. "I can take word, if ye want me to."

"That will do first-rate," answered Shep. "We can send word where some of the men can meet us—and in the meantime we can watch the lion, so that he doesn't get away, and doesn't die of hunger and thirst."

"Wild beasts can live a long time without food and drink," said Jed Sanborn. "But the gittin' away is another story. Better watch him putty closely."

After a good deal of talking the boys decided to return to their camp. It was arranged that the old hunter should depart for town at once, find out where the circus was, and inform the proprietor that the lion was found. Then, when a circus representative appeared, Sanborn was to meet him, arrange to cage the lion, and meet the boys at their camp, the location of which they described in such a manner that it could not be missed. Sanborn said the circus manager had found out that the three discharged employees were guilty of letting the animals escape, and the men were now in jail.

"Tell our folks that we are well and having a grand time," said Snap, and Sanborn promised to do so.

After a hearty dinner, at which the old hunter ate his fill of the things cooked by Giant, the boys and the old hunter separated, and Shep and his chums struck out for the camp. It was still warm, so the doctor's son did not mind the loss of his shirt. He had more at the camp, so the loss did not matter much.

"I am glad we saw Jed," said Shep as they trudged along. "That will save us the trip to town. I hope he gets the circus folks here soon."

"Tommy won't want to see them," said Giant. "He told me he never wanted to see the inside of a circus tent again."

"And I don't blame him," returned Snap. "Well, he can easily keep out of the way, and we needn't say anything about him."

"Wonder what he'll do after we go home?"

"I've got an idea," came from the doctor's son. "Let us take him with us and do what we can to find his sister. If we can't find her, let us see if we can't find a home for him and put him to school. He ought to get an education."

"I'm willing to do what I can," said Snap readily. His eyes brightened. "We might spend some of that reward for the lion on Tommy. I'd be willing to put in my share."

"So would I," answered Shep.

In the middle of the afternoon they reached a beauwul spot in the mountains, where a rocky stream formed a series of waterfalls. This locality had been mentioned by Dr. Reed, and they spent some time getting different pictures of it, Snap assisting the others, since he had no camera of his own.

"I hope I get that camera back," he said.

"We all hope that," returned Giant. "The wild man can keep my sock—I shouldn't want to touch it after he had it."

The water at the foot of the falls looked good for fishing, and Giant pleaded for permission to fish for a quarter of an hour or so. This was granted, and he promptly baited up and threw in. As a consequence he soon caught a beautiful brook trout, and several more followed.

"Wait; I'll take a snapshot of hauling in the next fish," said the doctor's son, and he succeeded in getting a view that later on turned out exceedingly well.

Not having anything else to do, Snap wandered down the brook for a distance of a hundred yards. He was on the point of turning back when he saw something at a distance, moving among the brushwood. He looked sharply for a moment and then discovered that it was a large black bear.

CHAPTER XXVIII

AFTER A BLACK BEAR

"Shep! Giant! Quick!"

"What's the matter, Snap?"

"A bear! Down the stream! Come on with the guns!" went on Snap excitedly. He had returned hot-footed to where he had left his chums and the firearms.

"Are you sure?" queried the doctor's son as he dropped his camera and grabbed up his shotgun.

"Dead certain—but I don't know how long he will stay there. Oh, if I had only had my gun with me!" groaned Snap. "I could have brought him down as easy as pie!"

"Aren't you going to take your camera?" asked Giant as he drew in his line and took both his photo outfit and his firearm.

"Yes, I forgot," said the doctor's son, and picked up his camera again. "Don't shoot till we get a snapshot," he said to Snap, who, gun in hand, was already off.

"All right; but we don't want to lose the bear," answered the other young hunter.

"Of course not!"

With Snap in the lead, the three boys sneaked swiftly but silently down the mountain brook until they came to the spot from which Snap had discovered the bear. Here they halted, and the others looked enquiringly at their leader.

"I saw him right over yonder," whispered Snap. "Go slow, now, or you'll scare him."

With bated breath the three young hunters advanced down the tiny stream. They gained the shelter of some dense brushwood and gazed around eagerly. Not a sign of a bear was to be seen anywhere.

"Maybe you were dreaming, Snap," murmured Giant.

"No, I wasn't—I saw him just as plain as day."

"Then he must have seen you running back to the pool, and he must have took out, too."

"Perhaps; but I was very careful to keep out of sight."

They advanced a little farther, and now saw ahead of them a slight hollow, where there was another waterfall, sheltered on either side by sharp rocks.

"There he is!" whispered the doctor's son excitedly, and pointed down to the pool at the foot of the falls. The black bear was there, getting a drink.

"We can't take a picture from here," said Giant disappointedly. "What shall we do—fire?"

"Oh, we ought to have a picture of him," pleaded Shep. "It would be just the thing for our collection."

"Let me suggest something," said Snap. "I haven't any camera, so I'll stay here. You two can make a half circle and come up below and kind of head the bear off. If he starts to run before you get ready I'll fire at him."

So it was agreed, and Shep and Giant hurried off without delay, making a wide detour through the woods and over the rocks. They could not help making a little noise, but this was, as they rightfully reasoned, drowned out by the falling of the waters.

In the meantime Snap kept careful watch of the bear. The animal took his time drinking, raising his head several times to look around him. But he did not turn his gaze upward, and consequently did not discover the young hunter, who stood with weapon aimed, ready to fire at a moment's warning.

Fully five minutes passed, and then the bear stretched himself and commenced to sniff the air. Then, of a sudden, he arose on his hind legs to get a better look at his surroundings.

"This is the time they ought to get their pictures," thought Snap.

An instant later he saw something fluttering in the bushes below the pool. Shep and Giant were there and had their cameras in action. The bear continued to stand upright, but presently he dropped on all fours and began to lumber away from the brook at a good rate of speed.

To have waited longer would have been foolish, and taking careful aim, Snap fired his shotgun twice. Scarcely had the two reports rung out than Giant also fired, followed, a few seconds later, by the doctor's son.

The aims of all three of the young hunters were true, and the bear received such a peppering of buckshot that he was seriously if not mortally wounded. He dropped down, dragged himself up again, and roared with rage and pain.

"Give him another!" yelled Snap as he started to reload.

Giant was the first to run into the opening, and as the bear saw the youth he snarled viciously and showed his teeth. He tried to rush at the boy, but Giant discharged the second barrel of his shotgun and the charge took the bear in the head. Then the doctor's son fired again, and hit the animal in the side. This was too much for bruin, and with a rocking motion he staggered forward a few steps and then pitched on his head, dead.

"We've got him! We've got him!" yelled the small youth, dancing around wildly and flinging his cap into the air. "Isn't this the dandy luck?"

"Did you get the pictures?" questioned Snap, leaping down the rocks to where the game lay.

"We sure did," answered the doctor's son. "And I've got one of you aiming your gun right at the bear. I tilted the camera up a little to get it."

"What a fine bear!" cried Giant.

"We never got a better," answered Snap. "Oh, this is certainly prime luck!"

"We'll have to take some more pictures—of our game," said Shep, and without delay they took several plates and films— the two cameras being of each kind. All the boys were in the pictures, and of these photographs they were justly proud.

"Now, the question is, what are we going to do with the bear?" said Snap. "We can't drag such a load to our camp."

"We'll have to skin the animal and take what meat we want," answered the doctor's son. "It's too bad to leave so much behind, but it can't be helped. It won't keep in this weather, anyway."

"If only Jed Sanborn was here—he might take some of

it home."

"I'll tell you what we can do," said Giant. "Try to drag the carcass—or a big part of it—up to the lion's pit. It will help to feed that beast until the circus folks come."

"That's an idea," said Shep. "And if we keep the lion well fed he won't try so hard to get away. Menagerie animals are always lazy when well fed—one of the keepers told me that. They only get restless when they are hungry."

It took the boys some time to skin the dead bear and cut away such meat as they thought they could tote along. The rest of the meat they hung in a tree, thinking they might possibly come back for it later. Then they started once more for camp.

"I hope the Spink crowd hasn't been bothering Whopper and Tommy since we have been away," said Snap. "If they have—"

"Don't borrow trouble," interrupted the doctor's son. "Wait till it comes."

With their heavy loads, they made slow progress through the woods, and they were glad when they reached the lion pit and could dispose of some of the bear meat. The lion greeted them with a roar, but that was all. He had not yet eaten the second wildcat; nevertheless, they threw to him a chunk of the bear meat, the fresh blood of which was very much to his satisfaction.

It was late when they reached camp, thoroughly tired out. Whopper and Tommy were glad to see them, and immediately bustled about to get them a good supper. Those left behind listened with interest to the tale the others had to tell. When Shep told about the tracks around the lonely cabin, tracks that had caused Jed Sanborn to ask if they had seen a dog, Tommy looked greatly interested.

"Say!" he cried. "Do you suppose—" And then he stopped short.

"Do we suppose what?" queried Shep.

"Oh, I suppose it couldn't be, but I was just thinking. Maybe that isn't a crazy man at all."

"Well, what do you think it can be?" asked Giant.

"Maybe it's Abe, the runaway chimpanzee."

CHAPTER XXIX

THE BOTTOM OF A MYSTERY

All the others listened to Tommy's words with interest. Then Whopper spoke of the face he had seen as looking particularly impish.

"It was pretty dark, so we couldn't see very well," said he. "It might have been the chimpanzee."

"Would that chimpanzee steal a watch, and a camera, and a gun?" demanded the doctor's son.

"He'll take whatever happens to interest him," answered the boy from the circus. "They are constantly trying to teach him new tricks. If you'll remember, one of his tricks is to fire a gun into the air. And another is to look at a watch and pretend to tell the time."

"That's so!" cried Snap. "I saw him do both at the show."

"Would he untie our boat?" asked Giant.

"He might."

"If it is the chimpanzee we'll have a hard job of it catching him," said Shep slowly. "He won't stay at the cabin, but roam from place to place—and there is no telling what he'll do with our things."

"Don't forget the reward that has been offered," said Giant. "If we can find the chimpanzee we can get that as well as the reward for the lion."

Whopper and Tommy had not been bothered by the Spink crowd, and were of the opinion that the latter had shifted their camp to a new locality, closer to the lake.

"Well, let them keep their distance, that's all I ask," said the doctor's son.

The next day Snap, Shep and Giant rested, while Whopper and Tommy went on a short hunt, bringing in some partridges and several squirrels. The boys took a few pictures, Snap using an extra camera that had been brought along. They now had a fine collection, of which they were exceedingly proud.

Sunday passed, and still they heard nothing from Jed Sanborn. The boys went hunting several times and brought in a variety of small game. They made a trip to the mountain-top and got several more photographs of value. Films and plates were carefully stored away in water-and-light-tight cases.

"I am sure my father will be greatly pleased when he sees what we have accomplished," said Shep. "I don't believe he thought we could do so well."

On Tuesday morning, just after breakfast, the young hunters heard somebody coming through the woods toward them. Wags set up a violent barking.

"Maybe it's Sanborn with the circus folks," said Whopper.

"Oh, what shall I do?" asked Tommy in alarm. "I don't want them to see me."

"It's the Spink crowd!" cried Giant. "Say, something must be wrong! Look how excited they are!"

"We ought to shoot 'em—that's what we ought to do!" they heard Carl Dudder say loudly.

"We'll make 'em pay for the things, that's what we'll make 'em do," answered Ham Spink.

"Call off your dog, you rascals!" sang out Dick Bush, for Wags had walked toward him, barking angrily.

"Come here, Wags!" cried Tommy, and the collie obeyed instantly. But he evidently knew that the newcomers were enemies, for he continued to eye them suspiciously.

"Think you're smart, don't you?" roared Ham Spink, striding into the camp and facing Shep and Snap. "Well, I want you to know that you have gone too far. You've got to pay damages, or we'll have you all locked up."

"You've got to pay for my new suit of clothes," said Ike Akley. "It is utterly ruined."

"And my sweater," said Dick Bush.

"And I want to know where my shoes are?" put in Carl Dudder. "And my briar-root pipe and tobacco."

"Yes, and my silver matchcase, and a whole lot of other things," said Ham Spink.

"Yes; and what right had you to make a roughhouse of our camp?" demanded another boy.

"All of our stores are ruined," put in still another.

"It was mean to scatter that coffee in the mud!"

"And the sugar and beans!"

"Yes; and put the salt in the flour!"

So the talk ran on, the newcomers getting more and more excited every moment. They had their guns with them, and looked as if they meant to do serious harm to our friends.

"See here, what are you talking about?" asked the doctor's son at last. "I can't make head or tail of it." He realized that something unusual had occurred.

This brought forth another volley of accusations from the Spink crowd. Their camp had been "rough-housed" to the last degree, and many things had been utterly ruined, while other articles were missing. They were sure that Shep and his chums were guilty of the crime.

"You are all wrong," cried Snap. "We haven't been near your camp."

"That's the truth," added Shep.

"I don't believe it," cried Carl Dudder.

"But it is true—every word of it," came from Giant, and Whopper and Tommy said the same.

"You've been there—and you have our things," said Ike Akley doggedly.

"If you want to do so, you can search this camp," said Shep. "But don't you harm any of our goods."

"Do you mean to say you didn't come to our camp last night?" demanded Ham.

"I certainly do say it," answered the doctor's son. "All we did was to hide that boat, and we did that because we knew you wanted to hide ours."

"Huh! How did you know that?"

"Because we heard you talking about it, on the way to the lake."

"Well, if you didn't come to our camp last night, who did?" asked Dick Bush. He was commencing to realize that a mistake had been made.

"Don't ask me," answered Snap. "But, honor bright, we weren't near your camp, Dick."

"Maybe it was the chimpanzee!" cried Tommy.

"Eh?" queried Ham.

In a few brief words the Spink crowd were told of what had happened at the cabin, at the cliff, and at the lake shore. No mention was made of the capture of the lion.

"We think it was the chimpanzee," said Snap. "But we may be mistaken—it may be a crazy man."

More talk followed, and in the end Snap and his chums agreed to visit the wrecked camp and take a look around. They left Tommy in charge of their own camp and warned him to keep strict guard.

It was a walk of half a mile, and the boys covered it in less than half an hour. Snap was in advance, with Ham by his side. Ham still thought our friends guilty of what had occurred.

"Here's our camp—or what's left of it," said Ham as they came to the clearing. "Now, if you—"

He stopped short and gazed ahead, with eyes bulging from his head. Snap gave a yell.

"Boys, here he is! The chimpanzee, and he's having a high old time!"

Captain Ralph Bonehill

All of the others rushed forward, and saw a sight that filled some with rage and others with laughter. Sure enough, Abe, the educated chimpanzee, was there, and was evidently having the time of his life. He had on a highly-colored dress shirt, a cap and one shoe, and was amusing himself by tearing a hunting suit belonging to Ham into shreds.

"The chimpanzee, sure enough!"

"Look what he is doing!"

"Shoot him! Shoot the rascal!"

So the cries rang out. The chimpanzee looked up in alarm. Then, as several guns were raised, he leaped out of sight behind some bushes and went off, chattering wildly as he disappeared.

CHAPTER XXX

GOOD-BY TO THE BOY HUNTERS

"I'll kill that monkey!" roared Ham as he ran into the camp and picked up his ruined clothing. "Look at this!"

"And this!" added Carl Dudder, snatching up the remains of his sleeping blanket.

"It was the chimpanzee, sure enough," said Dick Bush.

"Come on after him!" exclaimed Shep. "Remember the reward," he whispered to his chums.

All presently made off after the chimpanzee. They kept in a bunch at first, but gradually separated, the Spink crowd going one way and Snap and his chums in another.

"I'm glad we caught sight of him as we did," said Whopper. "Now those fellows know we were not guilty of the rough-housing."

"It certainly was rough," was Giant's comment. "Three-quarters of their things are ruined."

"Perhaps they can hold the circus proprietor responsible," said the doctor's son.

They moved forward for nearly a quarter of a mile, and were

on the point of giving up the search and returning to camp when Giant caught sight of a small, cave-like opening on the mountain side.

"Let's look in there," he said. "See, there is a vest on the ground in front of it!"

"Be careful—the chimpanzee may be dangerous!" warned Snap.

They hurried forward, with eyes and ears on the alert. Giant looked into the opening.

"No monkey here," he announced. "But he has been here. Look!"

And much to Snap's delight he held up the missing camera. Then he ran into the cave and came forth with Shep's watch, and a number of trinkets taken from the Spink camp.

"He must have come here after he left the old cabin," said Snap. "See, there is some food. He must have gotten that last night, when he raided Spink's place."

They took with them all the things to be found, and then made another search for the chimpanzee. But they could not locate the marauding creature, and so turned their steps toward their camp.

"Well, we've got a few of those others fellows' things for them," said Whopper. "We can return them after dinner."

"The camera is O.K.," said Snap, after an examination.

"And so is the watch," came from the doctor's son.

"And to think it was only a chimpanzee, after all!" cried Giant.

"'Only' is good!" exclaimed Shep. "He's had enough for

anybody, I'm thinking!"

As they came closer to their camp they heard Tommy talking in a loud voice to somebody. Wags was barking gaily.

"Now you sit still and behave yourself," the circus boy was saying. "Then you'll get a fine lump of sugar."

"Talking to the dog, I suppose," said Whopper. "He thinks Wags—No, he isn't, either. Well, I never! If this doesn't beat anything I ever saw!"

All came into the clearing and gazed in amazement at the sight presented. Chained to a tree was Abe, the chimpanzee, smiling and chattering, and in front of him were Tommy and the dog, the former with some sugar in his hand.

"Hullo!" cried Snap. "Did you catch him?"

"I certainly did!" answered the circus boy. "But I had the time of my life doing it. He ran up a tree, and he wouldn't come down until I offered him a handful of those nuts I found yesterday. They were too much of a temptation, and while I fed him nuts with one hand I took the kettle chain and tied him up as you see."

"Good for you!" said Whopper. "He must have known you, or I guess he would have run away."

"Yes, he started to run away, but I whistled like his keeper used to whistle, and that made him sit still."

"You want to make sure of that chain," said the doctor's son. "I see he has Snap's belt on," he added with a grin.

"I'll tie him with a rope," answered Tommy, and later the chimpanzee was firmly secured, so that escape was out of the question. As the young hunters fed him well, he seemed quite content.

"Tommy, this is an important capture for you," said Shep. "It's money in your pocket. The circus proprietor has offered five hundred dollars reward for the capture of this chimpanzee."

"Five hundred dollars!" gasped the little fellow. "But they won't pay it to me!" he added, as his face fell.

"We'll make them pay—if they want the animal," answered Snap.

"But I don't want them to see me," insisted Tommy.

"See here, Tommy, you leave this matter to us," said the doctor's son. "I don't think they can compel you to go with the circus. We'll take you to Fairview, and you can remain with us until we hear from your sister."

"All right; but if they take me I'll run away again," answered the boy.

A little later the Spink crowd came into camp and were astonished to learn of the capture of the chimpanzee. They were glad to get back the things that had been found, but declared that so many other articles had been ruined they would have to give up their outing.

"Let's be generous to them," whispered Shep to his chums. "I don't think we want to stay after the circus people come for the lion and the chimpanzee." And after some talking the young hunters offered the Spink crowd part of their food supplies and a few other things. This surprised Ham, Carl and the rest. They accepted the offer on the spot, and a better feeling prevailed between the boys than had for many months.

"It's very nice of you to do this," said Dick Bush. "I shan't forget it."

"I'm sorry I accused you of ruining the camp," came

from Ham.

"So am I," added Carl. "But—well, you know how it was."

"We'll let bygones be bygones," said the doctor's son. "It's better to be friends than enemies."

"I—I suppose so," said Ham humbly, and then he and his cronies took their departure.

The young hunters watched out for the reappearance of Jed Sanborn, Snap and Shep going to Firefly Lake for that purpose. Two days later they saw the old hunter coming to the shore with a big flat-bottomed boat, containing four men. The men were from the circus and said they had come for the captured lion.

"We want to make sure of that reward," said the doctor's son.

"All right, young man, turn the lion over to us and the money is yours," said one of the men. "But we'll want a receipt from all the boys who captured the beast."

"You'll get that," said Snap. "You offered a reward for the chimpanzee, too, didn't you?"

"Certainly; five hundred dollars."

"Well, we've got him, too."

"You have? How did you do it?" asked the man, and very briefly Snap related the tale, but did not give Tommy's name.

"That boy is in luck, for the half thousand is his," said the circus man. "Glad you got Abe," he added. "He is a great drawing-card and worth a dozen lions to us."

A visit was made to the lion pit, and after a good deal of trouble the lion was brought to the surface of the ground and chained and muzzled. One of the men knew the beast well and had little trouble in walking the lion to the lake shore, where he was chained to a tree, and left in charge of one of the party.

The circus men were vastly surprised when they learned that it was Tommy who had captured the chimpanzee. At first they did not think they ought to pay the lad the reward, but Shep told them they could not have Abe unless they did so.

"A bargain is a bargain," said the doctor's son. "You'll not touch the chimpanzee unless you pay up."

The matter was argued hotly, but in the end the circus men gave in, and two checks were made out, both payable to Dr. Reed, and the boys signed the receipts. Then the circus men took the chimpanzee, and walked down to the lake shore.

"Guess you don't want Tommy any more," cried Shep after them.

"No; we've got another kid to take his place," answered one of the men.

"They'll have their hands full getting that lion and the chimpanzee to town," said Snap, and he was right. But the work was accomplished by the next day, and the pair were shipped on to the circus by train.

The young hunters remained in camp forty-eight hours longer, and then packed up and moved down to Firefly Lake. Just previous to going they let the Spink crowd have some more of their things, for which the other lads were extremely grateful.

"Guess we better be friends after this," said Ham Spink. "It doesn't pay to be on the outs."

"It doesn't," answered Shep readily.

On the return to Fairview the boy hunters camped out three

nights, and shot a variety of small game and also a deer. They took the latter home and also the skin of the bear, which was afterward cured and is now on the floor of the Dodge parlor."

"You have done exceedingly well," said Dr. Reed, when he had heard their story and gone over their films and plates and pictures. "These will make a grand collection, and are just what we wanted for advertising purposes."

The money obtained for the capture of the lion was divided among the four boy hunters, and the amount received for the chimpanzee was placed to Tommy's credit by the doctor, and the former circus boy went to live with the Reed family for the time being. Several letters were sent to Tommy's missing sister, and at last word came back from her. She had married a storekeeper who was rich, and she asked that Tommy come to live with her.

"My, but that's grand!" cried Tommy. "Now I'll have a good home."

"I'm mighty glad of it," said Shep, and the other lads said the same. Later they received letters from Tommy stating that his sister and his brother-in-law treated him well and were going to give him a fine education.

"Well, it was a great outing," said Snap, one day, when the boy hunters were talking it over.

"We'll have to go out again some day," said Whopper.

"School for ours!" cried the doctor's son.

"Right you are," came from Giant. "But, say, we had a dandy time, didn't we?"

"So we did!" cried all the others; and here we will leave the four boy hunters and say good-by.

Choose from Thousands of 1stWorldLibrary Classics By

A. M. Barnard
Ada Leverson
Adolphus William Ward
Aesop
Agatha Christie
Alexander Aaronsohn
Alexander Kielland
Alexandre Dumas
Alfred Gatty
Alfred Ollivant
Alice Duer Miller
Alice Turner Curtis
Alice Dunbar
Allen Chapman
Alleyne Ireland
Ambrose Bierce
Amelia E. Barr
Amory H. Bradford
Andrew Lang
Andrew McFarland Davis
Andy Adams
Angela Brazil
Anna Alice Chapin
Anna Sewell
Annie Besant
Annie Hamilton Donnell
Annie Payson Call
Annie Roe Carr
Annonaymous
Anton Chekhov
Archibald Lee Fletcher
Arnold Bennett
Arthur C. Benson
Arthur Conan Doyle
Arthur M. Winfield
Arthur Ransome
Arthur Schnitzler
Arthur Train
Atticus
B.H. Baden-Powell
B. M. Bower
B. C. Chatterjee
Baroness Emmuska Orczy
Baroness Orczy
Basil King
Bayard Taylor
Ben Macomber
Bertha Muzzy Bower
Bjornstjerne Bjornson

Booth Tarkington
Boyd Cable
Bram Stoker
C. Collodi
C. E. Orr
C. M. Ingleby
Carolyn Wells
Catherine Parr Traill
Charles A. Eastman
Charles Amory Beach
Charles Dickens
Charles Dudley Warner
Charles Farrar Browne
Charles Ives
Charles Kingsley
Charles Klein
Charles Hanson Towne
Charles Lathrop Pack
Charles Romyn Dake
Charles Whibley
Charles Willing Beale
Charlotte M. Braeme
Charlotte M. Yonge
Charlotte Perkins Stetson
Clair W. Hayes
Clarence Day Jr.
Clarence E. Mulford
Clemence Housman
Confucius
Coningsby Dawson
Cornelis DeWitt Wilcox
Cyril Burleigh
D. H. Lawrence
Daniel Defoe
David Garnett
Dinah Craik
Don Carlos Janes
Donald Keyhoe
Dorothy Kilner
Dougan Clark
Douglas Fairbanks
E. Nesbit
E. P. Roe
E. Phillips Oppenheim
E. S. Brooks
Earl Barnes
Edgar Rice Burroughs
Edith Van Dyne
Edith Wharton

Edward Everett Hale
Edward J. O'Biren
Edward S. Ellis
Edwin L. Arnold
Eleanor Atkins
Eleanor Hallowell Abbott
Eliot Gregory
Elizabeth Gaskell
Elizabeth McCracken
Elizabeth Von Arnim
Ellem Key
Emerson Hough
Emilie F. Carlen
Emily Bronte
Emily Dickinson
Enid Bagnold
Enilor Macartney Lane
Erasmus W. Jones
Ernie Howard Pie
Ethel May Dell
Ethel Turner
Ethel Watts Mumford
Eugene Sue
Eugenie Foa
Eugene Wood
Eustace Hale Ball
Evelyn Everett-green
Everard Cotes
F. H. Cheley
F. J. Cross
F. Marion Crawford
Fannie E. Newberry
Federick Austin Ogg
Ferdinand Ossendowski
Fergus Hume
Florence A. Kilpatrick
Fremont B. Deering
Francis Bacon
Francis Darwin
Frances Hodgson Burnett
Frances Parkinson Keyes
Frank Gee Patchin
Frank Harris
Frank Jewett Mather
Frank L. Packard
Frank V. Webster
Frederic Stewart Isham
Frederick Trevor Hill
Frederick Winslow Taylor

Friedrich Kerst
Friedrich Nietzsche
Fyodor Dostoyevsky
G.A. Henty
G.K. Chesterton
Gabrielle E. Jackson
Garrett P. Serviss
Gaston Leroux
George A. Warren
George Ade
Geroge Bernard Shaw
George Cary Eggleston
George Durston
George Ebers
George Eliot
George Gissing
George MacDonald
George Meredith
George Orwell
George Sylvester Viereck
George Tucker
George W. Cable
George Wharton James
Gertrude Atherton
Gordon Casserly
Grace E. King
Grace Gallatin
Grace Greenwood
Grant Allen
Guillermo A. Sherwell
Gulielma Zollinger
Gustav Flaubert
H. A. Cody
H. B. Irving
H.C. Bailey
H. G. Wells
H. H. Munro
H. Irving Hancock
H. R. Naylor
H. Rider Haggard
H. W. C. Davis
Haldeman Julius
Hall Caine
Hamilton Wright Mabie
Hans Christian Andersen
Harold Avery
Harold McGrath
Harriet Beecher Stowe
Harry Castlemon
Harry Coghill
Harry Houdini

Hayden Carruth
Helent Hunt Jackson
Helen Nicolay
Hendrik Conscience
Hendy David Thoreau
Henri Barbusse
Henrik Ibsen
Henry Adams
Henry Ford
Henry Frost
Henry James
Henry Jones Ford
Henry Seton Merriman
Henry W Longfellow
Herbert A. Giles
Herbert Carter
Herbert N. Casson
Herman Hesse
Hildegard G. Frey
Homer
Honore De Balzac
Horace B. Day
Horace Walpole
Horatio Alger Jr.
Howard Pyle
Howard R. Garis
Hugh Lofting
Hugh Walpole
Humphry Ward
Ian Maclaren
Inez Haynes Gillmore
Irving Bacheller
Isabel Cecilia Williams
Isabel Hornibrook
Israel Abrahams
Ivan Turgenev
J.G.Austin
J. Henri Fabre
J. M. Barrie
J. M. Walsh
J. Macdonald Oxley
J. R. Miller
J. S. Fletcher
J. S. Knowles
J. Storer Clouston
J. W. Duffield
Jack London
Jacob Abbott
James Allen
James Andrews
James Baldwin

James Branch Cabell
James DeMille
James Joyce
James Lane Allen
James Lane Allen
James Oliver Curwood
James Oppenheim
James Otis
James R. Driscoll
Jane Abbott
Jane Austen
Jane L. Stewart
Janet Aldridge
Jens Peter Jacobsen
Jerome K. Jerome
Jessie Graham Flower
John Buchan
John Burroughs
John Cournos
John F. Kennedy
John Gay
John Glasworthy
John Habberton
John Joy Bell
John Kendrick Bangs
John Milton
John Philip Sousa
John Taintor Foote
Jonas Lauritz Idemil Lie
Jonathan Swift
Joseph A. Altsheler
Joseph Carey
Joseph Conrad
Joseph E. Badger Jr
Joseph Hergesheimer
Joseph Jacobs
Jules Vernes
Julian Hawthrone
Julie A Lippmann
Justin Huntly McCarthy
Kakuzo Okakura
Karle Wilson Baker
Kate Chopin
Kenneth Grahame
Kenneth McGaffey
Kate Langley Bosher
Kate Langley Bosher
Katherine Cecil Thurston
Katherine Stokes
L. A. Abbot
L. T. Meade

L. Frank Baum
Latta Griswold
Laura Dent Crane
Laura Lee Hope
Laurence Housman
Lawrence Beasley
Leo Tolstoy
Leonid Andreyev
Lewis Carroll
Lewis Sperry Chafer
Lilian Bell
Lloyd Osbourne
Louis Hughes
Louis Joseph Vance
Louis Tracy
Louisa May Alcott
Lucy Fitch Perkins
Lucy Maud Montgomery
Luther Benson
Lydia Miller Middleton
Lyndon Orr
M. Corvus
M. H. Adams
Margaret E. Sangster
Margret Howth
Margaret Vandercook
Margaret W. Hungerford
Margret Penrose
Maria Edgeworth
Maria Thompson Daviess
Mariano Azuela
Marion Polk Angellotti
Mark Overton
Mark Twain
Mary Austin
Mary Catherine Crowley
Mary Cole
Mary Hastings Bradley
Mary Roberts Rinehart
Mary Rowlandson
M. Wollstonecraft Shelley
Maud Lindsay
Max Beerbohm
Myra Kelly
Nathaniel Hawthrone
Nicolo Machiavelli
O. F. Walton
Oscar Wilde
Owen Johnson
P.G. Wodehouse
Paul and Mabel Thorne

Paul G. Tomlinson
Paul Severing
Percy Brebner
Percy Keese Fitzhugh
Peter B. Kyne
Plato
Quincy Allen
R. Derby Holmes
R. L. Stevenson
R. S. Ball
Rabindranath Tagore
Rahul Alvares
Ralph Bonehill
Ralph Henry Barbour
Ralph Victor
Ralph Waldo Emmerson
Rene Descartes
Ray Cummings
Rex Beach
Rex E. Beach
Richard Harding Davis
Richard Jefferies
Richard Le Gallienne
Robert Barr
Robert Frost
Robert Gordon Anderson
Robert L. Drake
Robert Lansing
Robert Lynd
Robert Michael Ballantyne
Robert W. Chambers
Rosa Nouchette Carey
Rudyard Kipling
Saint Augustine
Samuel B. Allison
Samuel Hopkins Adams
Sarah Bernhardt
Sarah C. Hallowell
Selma Lagerlof
Sherwood Anderson
Sigmund Freud
Standish O'Grady
Stanley Weyman
Stella Benson
Stella M. Francis
Stephen Crane
Stewart Edward White
Stijn Streuvels
Swami Abhedananda
Swami Parmananda
T. S. Ackland

T. S. Arthur
The Princess Der Ling
Thomas A. Janvier
Thomas A Kempis
Thomas Anderton
Thomas Bailey Aldrich
Thomas Bulfinch
Thomas De Quincey
Thomas Dixon
Thomas H. Huxley
Thomas Hardy
Thomas More
Thornton W. Burgess
U. S. Grant
Upton Sinclair
Valentine Williams
Various Authors
Vaughan Kester
Victor Appleton
Victor G. Durham
Victoria Cross
Virginia Woolf
Wadsworth Camp
Walter Camp
Walter Scott
Washington Irving
Wilbur Lawton
Wilkie Collins
Willa Cather
Willard F. Baker
William Dean Howells
William le Queux
W. Makepeace Thackeray
William W. Walter
William Shakespeare
Winston Churchill
Yei Theodora Ozaki
Yogi Ramacharaka
Young E. Allison
Zane Grey

www.ingramcontent.com/pod-product-compliance
Lightning Source LLC
Chambersburg PA
CBHW030307180626
46810CB00003B/952